OISCARD

ROADSHOW

A RINEHART SUSPENSE NOVEL

A RINEHART SUSPENSE NOVEL

ROADSHOW

A Yellowthread Street Mystery

WILLIAM MARSHALL

Holt, Rinehart and Winston
New York

Published in the United States by
Holt, Rinehart and Winston,
383 Madison Avenue, New York, New York 10017.

Library of Congress Cataloging in Publication Data

Marshall, William Leonard, 1944–
Roadshow.

(A Yellowthread Street mystery) (A Rinehart
suspense novel)
I. Title.   II. Series: Marshall, William
Leonard, 1944–   . Yellowthread Street
mystery.
PR9619.3.M275R6   1985   823   85-858
ISBN 0-03-001744-0

First American Edition

Printed in Great Britain

1 3 5 7 9 10 8 6 4 2

ISBN 0-03-001744-0

The Hong Bay district of Hong Kong is
fictitious as are the people who, for
one reason or another, inhabit it.

FAUX PAS

Wait . . . wait . . . *wait* . . .

The trick was to know when, exactly, to . . .

Wait . . . wait . . .

At the corner of Isandula Street, at exactly 5.08 a.m., The Embarrassment Man said softly to himself in Cantonese, 'Wait . . . wait . . .'

He detected a movement: the faintest creaking of springs and leather under posteriors, the tiniest sound of a whisper.

Behind the tinted glass of the Mini parked out of the glow of the street lamp, he heard the first of all signs, The Rustle.

The Embarrassment Man's eyes stayed straight ahead, gazing down the street. He was not watching the car. His attention was on a group of four or five overalled and dust masked workmen searching for a gas leak at the far end of the road before the traffic started.

Another rustle.

He heard it. And then, after a little creaking, a whisper. He listened. The whisper was interrogative. The Embarrassment Man, rocking back a little on his heels, put his hand in the pocket of his khaki shorts and touched at his money.

So far so good.

It was a cool, dark morning. At the other end of the street the workmen unhurriedly began erecting some sort of rope barrier

I

in front of their truck and stringing it out across the road to cordon it off.

From inside the car, there was the whisper again. This time, it was interrogative tinged with alarm.

He was all right.

It was Male and Female. He heard a catch in the whispers, estimated the octaves, and sexed them.

In the embarrassment trade there were nodders, head incliners, cluckers and gazers depending on the level of competence, but The Embarrassment Man, a master practitioner, was none of those. The Embarrassment Man was a There.

The Embarrassment Man's attention stayed apparently on the workmen down the road, but inside the car, they knew where The Embarrassment Man's attention really was.

It was There.

The Embarrassment Man, the Marcel Marceau of the blush world, took a single step backwards on his bare feet and, a little uncomfortably, rubbed his sole against the back of his left leg. He was a child squirming at a sight meant to be spared the eyes of children. He inclined his head, not the way the Head Incliners did it (smarmily) but in a little glance downwards of sadness, a disappointment at the discovery of the loss of innocence in the world.

The Embarrassment Man, ten feet back from the car, his entire attention and body on the workmen down the road, concentrated his mind and listened.

He heard a click.

His brow furrowed. The click was a bad sign. It meant the car door was about to be flung open.

The Embarrassment Man took his hand out of his pocket and let his shoulders sink: body language. It meant he was a poor old man that no young Male canoodling in a car after dark could beat the shit out of without suffering the disapproval of the Female he was canoodling with.

Human nature. He knew it backwards.

The Embarrassment Man, turning in their direction as the workmen down the road went about their work, drew a shallow breath, held it, and then, as he folded his hands across his stomach, let the breath out with a pathetic, plaster saint-like upward rolling of his eyes.

The click turned into a creak as the pressure on the car door handle came off and the Male, at the whispered entreaty of his extra- or pre-marital mate, rubbed at his chin and tried to think of what to do next.

The Embarrassment Man took a single step forward.

It was the dangerous part. One wrong move and the Male would crack and the car and its customers would disappear in a sudden wrenching at the hand brake and a flurry of gear changing and engine starting.

He had to be quick.

The Embarrassment Man, casually, gazing around at the lightening sky, wondering merely what this day in Hong Kong might hold for all those who ventured out in it, looked hard at the licence plate.

The car, almost visibly, sagged.

Wonderful trade, glorious. The perfect high return business. All it took was pure genius. People he knew who knew people who could read always told him he should write a book.

A whisper. The Female. It was getting desperate.

The Embarrassment Man waited.

Wait . . . wait . . .

A click. This time, more subdued, softer. The Male had turned into the Boy and he was pushing down on the car door handle gently, respectfully, so as not to frighten The Embarrassment Man off so he could get out to reason with him.

The Embarrassment Man, gazing at the car, drew another breath and the sound stopped.

He was playing with them. The Embarrassment Man looked up at the sky.

Dawn was coming: he was considering whether or not to disappear into the multitude of Hong Kong taking his secret and the car number plate with him.

3

A little louder, he sighed . . .

The woman's voice said in urgent, loud Cantonese, 'Pay him!' She said something else, but The Embarrassment Man could not make it out. The woman's voice said in a shocked gasp, 'You told me you loved me!'

Ah, life . . . The Embarrassment Man, becoming aware of the presence of the car for the first time, looked over to the tinted windows with raised eyebrows. He wondered if anything was wrong.

He heard in Cantonese, '*I do love you.*'

The Embarrassment Man, ever the good citizen, took a step towards the car with the faintest of pleasant, concerned smiles on his face to see if he could help.

He heard the woman say, 'Pay him and let's –'

He heard the man say, 'I told my wife that I was –'

A lover and his lass. The Embarrassment Man, pausing, looked down the road. His finger to his lips, he pondered. He looked back to the sounds coming from the car. He blinked and looked moronic, smiled, craned a little forward, glanced again at the licence plate, and then . . .

You had to hand it to women. They knew their parts. The woman's voice said in sudden, frustrated hysteria, 'You stupid idiot, he's wondering whether or not he should call the *police*!'

The Male, like all Males everywhere, hesitated. The Embarrassment Man saw the car rock a little on its springs as his posterior moved, first, to get out, then changed direction and stayed to talk reason, then, seeing the woman's face, started to get out again, and then, deciding he was being shafted, moved again.

'Pay him!'

The Embarrassment Man looking again, helpfully moronic, took another step forward.

'Pay him! Pay him! Pay him!'

In a way, he was helping innocent womankind recognize the true intent of honeyed words.

The woman said, 'If that's all you think of me –!'

4

Licence plate, licence plate. This was where life could get difficult. One false step, the tiniest relaxation of role, the faintest knowing smile, and you could end up where the last Embarrassment Man to have had Isandula Street on his beat had ended up: on Isandula Street, up-ended and beaten.

The Embarrassment Man began slowly counting off numbers on the licence plate on his fingers, trying hard with all his might to etch the strange, unfamiliar symbols into his mind.

He waited.

Death now or glory.

He waited.

Slowly the car window came down.

Down the street, the overalled and dust masked workmen located their underground pipe and began marking it out in a line with what looked like silver paint tins strung together with rope.   ,

The Embarrassment Man, taking a single cautious step sideways towards the car, steeled himself.

He heard the car window make a soft bumping noise as it rolled down into the door frame.

He heard . . .

The Embarrassment Man, touching his fingertips together, turned slowly to say . . .

A voice from the car said meekly in Cantonese, 'Good morning.' In the street cold dawn was coming up. The Embarrassment Man could almost see the steam and warmth flow out from inside the car interior. The voice said, 'Um –' (A female whisper said in a harsh order, '*Pay him!*')

The Embarrassment Man, not turning to look – too discreet to intrude – opened his mouth to say –

The male voice said violently, 'Here!' The Embarrassment Man put out his hand and took the money. The male voice said in a hum as the engine started, 'Thanks! Thanks very much!'

The Embarrassment Man smiled. Ten dollars. Down the

road the workmen had got back into their truck and as the Mini did a U-turn in the street, The Embarrassment Man, as always, received not a single, one hand clap round of applause.

Well, that was the hard world of business.

The Embarrassment Man, shaking his head, blinked as the Mini paused at the edge of the cordon and began to do a U-turn. The workers' truck seemed to have gone and the Mini driver, not wanting to return to pass his way again, was moving backwards and forwards a little as he tried to decide which way to go.

The Embarrassment Man, not one to be an embarrassment, put his money in his pocket and, turning to walk to the corner, thought he might call it a night.

What the entire world needed was a nice little business returning a maximum of profit for a minimum of capital.

The Embarrassment Man had it.

The Embarrassment Man, smiling to himself, took a single step away in the direction of the waterfront. He glanced back and something was in the air, turning over and over.

He glanced back and there was a sheet, a wall, of thick black smoke rushing upwards and covering the turning car, enveloping it.

He glanced back and saw the flash, glanced back, saw the blast, the shock wave. It was all happening over and over, the car turning, spinning, somersaulting as it hit the pavement and flew to pieces. He saw the roadway itself coming up. He saw the tar and the bricks rising, turning over and over, shattering into dust. He saw – ·

He saw the entire street dissolve into a single shattering blast of blinding white light. He saw –

Falling, going over, losing his balance, being propelled backwards, his mouth open and screaming in terror, he saw –

Screaming, shouting, all his art forgotten, The Embarrassment Man clawed and ripped at the air in helpless incomprehension as the street, blown to pieces, in a single instant turned into a wave of rushing water and engulfed him.

It was 5.19 a.m. in Isandula Street, Hong Bay, British

Crown Colony of Hong Kong. It was a chill, Autumn morning, before dawn.

It was a few minutes before the first light of day.

It was only the beginning.

I

Hong Kong is an island of some thirty square miles under British administration in the South China Sea facing the Kowloon and New Territories area of continental China. Kowloon and the New Territories are also British administered, surrounded by the Communist Chinese province of Kwantung. The climate is generally sub-tropical, with hot, humid summers and high rainfall. The population of Hong Kong and the surrounding areas at any one time, including tourists and visitors, is in excess of five millions. The New Territories are leased from the Chinese. The lease is due to expire in 1997, but the British nevertheless maintain a military presence along the border, although, should the Communists, who supply almost all the colony's drinking water, ever desire to terminate the lease early, they need only turn off the taps. Hong Bay is on the southern side of the island and the tourist brochures advise you not to go there after dark.

Mongrel, half caste, unwanted, unloved, misunderstood, mangy, moth-eaten, flea-bitten, ragged, miserable, matted, tatty and abandoned.

In the Detectives' Room of the Yellowthread Street police station, the Man Without Pity was on duty and the dog, gazing up at him from the floor and slobbering onto the apple green ancient linoleum, didn't have a hope in Hell. From his desk,

Detective Senior Inspector Christopher Kwan O'Yee, pulling out a form from his top drawer, said as unfeeling stone, 'Tough shit, dog.' He fixed it with a steely eye. It was a little after 6 a.m. By 9, when the pound opened, the dog would be in the pound seeing half a dozen potential new owners. By 9.30, when half a dozen potential new owners had seen the dog, the dog would be in Death Row about to see the needle. By 1 p.m., when the needling started . . .

Right. Settled. Finito. Done. O'Yee said, 'Look at you! You're revolting!' He wrote in the first space on the form where it said Type Of Animal: *Dog*. O'Yee said, 'Who the hell's going to want you looking like that?' He looked at the dog and saw the head of what appeared to be some sort of Alsatian with spaniel ears on the body of a large, unwashed brown mop. O'Yee said, 'Right?' O'Yee said, 'Right!' He wrote in the space provided for Disposition: *Sudden Death*. O'Yee said to the dog, 'You've picked the wrong cop to wander in on. Bill Spencer: well, maybe you'd get away with it with him or maybe even Harry Feiffer, but me, never.' It was a truly disgusting dog. 'Boy, did you get a wrong number. You picked a bloody Eurasian. If you'd picked one of the others – one of the Europeans like Feiffer or Spencer, or one of the Chinese uniformed coppers in the charge room – you might have got away with being a poor, mixed up bloody mongrel, but with me you get zip.' O'Yee, leaning a little forward on his desk, said conspiratorially, 'Listen, dumbo, the whole point about feeling guilty about being rotten to people of mixed race is that you've got to start off from a guilt position of being pure bred yourself.' As well as being ugly, the dog was stupid. O'Yee said, 'Well, it's too late now.' He wrote in the space for Despatching Officer: *D.S.I. O'Yee* and signed at the bottom with a flourish.

Outside, the day was warming up. There wasn't even a bit of snow to make the thing work. The dog, wandering in off the street, had simply fallen down on the floor and started slobbering over the linoleum. Dogs in kids' movies or in Norman Rockwell drawings at least knew how to do Cute. This one didn't even know how to do Sentient. O'Yee said, 'You're for the chop and there's nothing I can do – or I even want to do about it.' O'Yee said, 'O.K.?' O'Yee said, 'For Christ's sake, can't you at least get up and lick my hand or something?'

It was 6.02. O'Yee, averting his gaze, signed the form again. The second signature made the form invalid. He took out another. O'Yee said reasonably, 'Look, even if I wanted to, I couldn't take you home. I live in an apartment and –' The dog gazed up at him. It was the worst looking dog he had ever seen in his life. 'And even if I didn't, my wife and children are in America with my relations so there'd be no one at home to even feed you.' O'Yee, shrugging, said, 'So there.' Settled. Right. Done. O'Yee, still shrugging, said, 'They – ah –' He pursed his lips, 'Look, they won't be back for at least another six weeks so even if I –'

O'Yee said, 'For the last three weeks I've been practically living here at the Station.' The clock still read 6.02. 'I mean, look at the time. I shouldn't even be here! North Point Station should be handling all our calls. In theory, we shouldn't even be open. The only reason I'm here at all is that – that I practically – well, since my family –' O'Yee said, 'You're better off dead.'

6.03. O'Yee said, 'I'll say this for you: you don't try and play on a person's sympathies. You take the blows as they come.' Needle city was just down the road. O'Yee said with a sneaking admiration, 'We mongs can't afford to demand too much from people or they –' O'Yee said, 'No, you're for it. You're not going to get to me like that. You're for the big sleep and that's it.' He took out another form and wrote in the space where it said Type Of Animal: *Dog* and in the space where it said Disposition . . .

The dog blinked not an eyelid.

Disposition . . .

Mongrel, half caste, unwanted, unloved, misunderstood, mangy, moth-eaten, ragged, miserable, matted, tatty and abandoned.

And the dog was even worse.

O'Yee said softly. 'O.K.'

The dog looked up at him. He didn't lick his hand.

O'Yee said, '*All right.*'

Outside, the day was starting: warm, balmy, and, as it had been for the last three weeks and would be for the next six, unbearably lonely.

Disposition: . . .

O'Yee said, 'Look.' O'Yee said, 'I'm a family man, O.K.?' He screwed up the form and held it for the dog to see.

O'Yee, desperate, said anxiously, 'O.K. see? All right?'

O'Yee said, 'Don't worry.' He leant down and touched the dog on the ear. O'Yee said in a whisper, 'Trust me. I'll think of *something* . . .'

In the back of the Bomb Squad truck at the far end of Isandula Street, the Mini driver said softly in Cantonese, 'What are my children going to think?' He had a cigarette in his hand. It was shaking. Inside the dark, tool and equipment lined truck, the smoke was going up towards the darkness of the ceiling and spreading. It was one of Detective Chief Inspector Harry Feiffer's cigarettes. Compared to the expensive after shave still lingering on the man's face it smelled very cheap. The Mini driver was a short, prosperous southern Chinese wearing what looked like a hand tailored Batik hang-out shirt. The shirt was covered in mud. The Mini driver, looking at the cigarette and seeming unable to decide whether to put it in his mouth or simply let the smoke curl, asked, shaking his head, 'Is she all right? The girl?'

Outside in the street the water had been turned off and there was only the sound of the storm drains taking away the overflow. There was a Department Of Main Roads bulldozer working to clear the eight foot deep hole the explosives had blown in the road so the pipe gangs could get at the fractured water main, but the bulldozer was far away and the sound came only as a steady drone.

'You were both lucky.' Outside, through the open doors of the truck, Feiffer could see the police photographers moving about the Mini to get shots of it from every conceivable angle. Caked solid in mud, there weren't too many angles to be found. Feiffer said softly, 'She's at the hospital with a few bruises. You were hit by a wall of mud and water. The mud cushioned the impact when you turned over.' He saw the Mini driver's eyes fall on The Embarrassment Man with Constable Lee a little off from the back door of the van. 'Tell me your name.'

'I didn't see anything. All I saw –' The Mini driver looked at The Embarrassment Man. 'You know who he is, don't you?' The Mini driver's hands tightened. The cigarette was wedged between his fingers. It shook with the force. The Mini driver said, 'You know what he is, don't you?' He looked hard into Feiffer's face without seeing it, 'People like you. Cops. European cops in Hong Kong! People who have been here a long time. I know people like you – you study people. You learn things – you – you take an interest.' The Mini driver, beginning to rise, demanded, 'You know what he is, don't you?'

Feiffer said again, 'Tell me your name.'

'You know what people like him do!' The Mini driver said, 'Lin. My name is Lin. I have a wife and three children and I have my entire family here in Hong Kong and I'm trying to build up a wholesale electronics business that my family have invested in because they believed in my integrity.' The Mini driver said, 'What harm was I doing? I work like a dog.' The Mini driver said, 'Lousy bitch! I didn't want to pay him. I knew what he was doing but she – she had to make me pay him and then –' He said softly, 'I'm finished. That's it. Everything I worked for.' He closed his eyes to cry but no tears came. The Mini driver said, 'Why don't you arrest him? Why don't you arrest people like that? What the hell do you think my taxes are for if you don't keep people like him off the streets?' He said before Feiffer could ask, 'She's one of the girls from my factory. All right? Is that what you want to know?'

'What I want to know is what you saw on the road.'

'I didn't see anything on the road. All I saw on the road was a cordon with men working behind it and then –' The Mini

13

driver said, 'All I had to do was just – I didn't see anything.' He demanded, 'Ask him – ask your little friend out there on the road what he saw!'

'How many workmen?'

'I don't know.'

'Two? Three? More?'

'I don't know.' Outside, The Embarrassment Man was giving a statement to P.C. Lee. From time to time Lee looked up from his notebook to shake his head or check something. The Mini driver said, 'Why the fuck is he still walking around? I thought you people put people like him in jail.' Maybe he wasn't getting through. The Mini driver said, 'He's an Embarrassment Man and he was looking at a man and a woman in a parked car.' He wasn't getting through. The Mini driver said suddenly in English, 'He's a fucking pervert. Does that make it clear enough for you?'

'What about a vehicle? A truck, or –'

'What are you trying to do – spare his feelings?' The Mini driver said, 'I know people like you –'

'No, you don't.'

'– don't I? I know Europeans like you who come here to study all about the picturesque Chinese and then fall in love with them so much that you'll forgive them anything!' He was rocking backwards and forwards, 'Well, I'm a real fucking Chinese and I know bastards like that and there's nothing picturesque about them because they're—' The tears were coming. The Mini driver said without any force, 'I know people like you who go to the trouble to learn perfect Cantonese and then –' The Mini driver, all the colour drained from his face, gazed up at the smoke on the roof of the truck and touched at his forehead with his fingers. He smelled his own after-shave. The Mini driver, sniffing, said desperately in Chinese, 'What am I going to do?'

There was nothing to say. He had seen nothing and there was nothing more to ask him. Feiffer, taking the burning cigarette from him and stubbing it out on the metal floor of the chassis, said quietly, 'It's all right. You're alive.' Outside, in the street, there was a gaping hole where someone had carefully and calculatedly blown a water main apart six feet below the earth and flooded a street. Feiffer said, 'One of my officers will take you home.' He saw the man about to say something. 'As a matter of fact, I didn't come here to learn all about the Chinese. I was born here in Hong Kong. I spoke Cantonese before I spoke English.'

The Mini driver shook his head. He wanted to cry, but there were no tears. The Mini driver, looking at The Embarrassment Man in the street, said – He stopped. There was something odd about the way The Embarrassment Man kept looking in the direction of the truck with the same strange, lost expression on his face he had had at the car, almost as if he was trying to find something he had misplaced. The Mini driver said – The Mini driver, suddenly understanding, said, 'No. Oh, no!' He looked at Feiffer's face and saw that it was true.

It was The Embarrassment Man's ultimate defence. In his repertoire, his finest, his greatest attribute and, unlike his friend Kam whom they had found one morning in the street almost beaten to death, it had kept him alive, out of trouble and at the top of his profession for a very long time.

Cataracts. In the early morning light, as he seemed to look around again for whatever it was he thought he had lost, The Embarrassment Man's eyes were milky and dull, nearly useless for more than shadows and movement at anything more than six feet.

He always stood no closer than seven feet six inches to any car he was covering.

The Mini driver, hiding his face in his hands, said 'NO.'

In the street, The Embarrassment Man heard his voice and, glad that he and the girl were still alive, smiled encouragingly in his direction.

It was 7.03 a.m. on the first day.

There was no rhyme or reason to it.

So far, for all the effort expended in Isandula Street, not one tangible result seemed to have been achieved.

*

15

At 7.04 a.m. in General Gordon Street, Police Constable Number 69162 Lo Kai Sun yelled through the miasma of diesel smoke of the early morning traffic to a fat Northern Chinese driving a Mercedes, 'Hey!' The fat Northern Chinese ignored him and started to turn his Mercedes towards him. Lo yelled in Cantonese, 'No, you don't. There's nothing wrong with your vehicle. *You keep moving.*' Lo, the single sentinel at the edge of chaos in the gutter, waved his hand to keep the flow going. He had seen that one before: the old overheating trick. Lo yelled as the driver went past at the traffic's top speed of three crawling miles an hour, 'You try that again and you'll find your vehicle in the police pound for sale back to you with a price tag of two thousand dollars on it!' Protecting the parking meters against 7–8 a.m. rush hour illegal use, Lo, resplendent in his knife edged crease khaki shirt and shorts and shining Sam Browne belt and holster, put his white gloved hand on a meter and dared someone to try to come and use it.

No one dared.

Once, someone had worked out in Traffic that with all the cars, taxis, trucks, vans and buses all out on the road at the same time there were five hundred and fifty feet of cars, taxis, trucks, vans and buses for every tenth of a mile of road. Someone had also worked out that that came to six hundred and fifty feet to road. Between the hours of 7 a.m. and 8 a.m. that calculation was conservative. Lo, assaulted by a fusillade of honking, tooting and bicycle bell ringing, stepped out onto the roadway and, weaving and pirouetting like Nureyev, got to a taxi about to do the old flat tyre routine.

They were all after his meters. At the bonnet of the taxi, Lo, like Death, smiled a thin smile and looked down meaningfully at the so-called flat tyre. The so-called flat tyre had been made to look flat by the simple expedient of not filling it with enough air. Lo may have looked young and clean-cut and handsome, but that was only on the outside. Lo, putting his gloved hand on the open window of the cab, said in an old, seedy, and ugly traffic cop's voice, 'Try to park at one of these meters at this time of morning, you child molester, and I'll hang your balls on my belt as a trophy.' There was a bicycle a little behind the cab with a black pyjama-suited old woman weaving and bobbing as the carbon monoxide played havoc with her ancient lungs. She was going for one of the parking spots. Lo, giving her a shove to keep her on her way, said in a snarl, 'Nice try, grandmother, but forget it.'

There was nothing wrong with her lungs. The old woman, spitting, shouted at top volume, 'It isn't illegal to –'

Oh, yes, it was. Lo, almost knocking her off her saddle as he moved further into the forest of moving metal to get a truck driver playing with the choke of his engine to pretend there was something wrong with his fuel pump, yelled, *'Keep moving.'*

The truck driver gave up the old choke-pulling routine and decided to do the my steering is going and I have to stop at one of the parking meters to fix it line. The only place he was going to stop if he stopped at one of the parking meters was in Stanley Prison on bread and water.

Lo, raising his voice to try and get it through thick heads that he was there to protect them against themselves, yelled to all and sundry, 'Peak hour! Clearway! No one stops until 8 a.m.!' He saw a bland looking man in his forties at the wheel of a Mazda sedan give him a nod and a friendly smile, a law and order supporter, and before he could turn out of the stream to just quietly tootle over to a parking meter to tell the traffic policeman sweating in the middle of the street just how much he supported the police and the work they did, Lo got his fist against the car's door and gave it a bash that almost stoved it in.

The police supporter yelled from behind the safety of his window, 'Fucking, officious, arsehole *cop.*'

The ads in the papers said it was a man's life policing at the crossroads of the world. They had only lied about there being crossroads. Lo, turning to face another barrage of honking, hooting and bell-ringing, took a mental note of the police supporter's number and filed it away under revenge.

Getting back to the sidewalk he glanced up and down

the street. Along the line of General Gordon Street's left hand gutter there were no less than thirty wonderfully empty metered parking bays. So far, they were still all virgins. Lo, stepping back off the roadway and putting his hands on his hips, nodded to himself. Life was great. He was doing something useful. The heart and arteries of the great city were throbbing and he – Chief Inspector Kyle-Foxby had used the expression in Lecture Two of the Traffic Fines Course – he was a good germ swimming along the bloodstream to clobber the bad germs. Also, he could abuse people that every code or philosophy the Chinese had followed for two millenniums said he wasn't allowed to abuse. With traffic you knew where you were: there were fines for everything. At his feet, there was a reinforced plastic hose running the full length of the parking meters, nestling up against their bases, and then disappearing into a little hole in the gutter, with a sign on the hose reading *Traffic Evaluation Experiment Penalty for Removal $200*, and he gave it a little stroke with his shoe to show it that it was well protected.

A car out in the stream of traffic gave a sudden lurch as an elderly driver had a heart attack and tried to veer off to find a safe spot against one of the meters to die. He saw Lo. He decided not to die. The dying man yelled out, 'May your balls turn to butter.' He goggled, swerved, and almost piled up as, in front of him, a grizzled, bare-chested rickshaw puller, dripping sweat, suddenly lurched to turn left. The man, with muscles on his legs like balloons, was at the end of a very long life pulling passengers and, as the gods called him to his final rest, he thought he might just drop off his three hundred pounds of paying human flesh in front of one of the parking meters on his way to a well-earned rest with the bones of his Confucian ancestors. Lo was also a Confucian: he understood about respect for the old. Lo, waving his hands and standing in front of the about-to-be-assaulted meter like a shotgun carrying father, shrieked, 'Come anywhere near this meter, you lousy old fart and I'll run you in for blocking traffic and bringing the entire Colony to a halt!' The rickshaw puller gave him a forlorn, sad, grandfatherly look. Lo gave him a cop's look. A posse of old-men-pulling-rickshaws supporters treated him to a fusillade of honking and hooting and bell ringing and Lo, immovable, yelled back, 'I'm a good germ! I'm keeping the traffic going!'

The only good Germ was a dead Germ. Lo, the only thing between flow and foul-up, between peak-hour and pandemonium, yelled as he went back into the centre of the road, 'Keep it moving! Keep it moving!'

It was awful, ghastly, man's worst modern nightmare: the ultimate expression of the ant running hopelessly, uselessly, and totally pointlessly around and round in ever decreasing circles. It was traffic.

And, at 7.09 a.m. when it was at its absolute Hong Kong's world's worst, taking time off from waving his arms and shouting orders only to land a kick on the immaculate coach work of a Rolls Royce driving for the meters under what it foolishly thought was the protection of a gubernatorial standard, Police Constable Number 69162 Lo loved every moment of it.

What they had after the bulldozer had cleared the area and the water had been pumped out of the hole was a gaping wound almost eight feet deep and twenty-two feet long in the surface of the street.

What they had was a hole. At the rim, Detective Chief Inspector Harry Feiffer said in expectation, 'Well?' He waited to see what, according to the Bomb Squad, the Department Of Main Roads, and the men from Public Works, Fingerprints and Scientific, the hole was supposed to represent. From the silence and the lack of eager, upturned faces from the hole, what it represented was a hole. The Hong Bay field operations man from the Main Roads Department was nearest to him in the hole and Feiffer, squatting down to catch his attention, asked, 'Well?'

By the Main Roads man there was nothing but the shattered and powdered jagged edge of the three foot bore water pipe the blast seemed to have been aimed at. The water pipe had carried only water. Feiffer, leaning a little further forward over the excavation, said again, patiently, 'Well?'

'Well what?'

The Main Roads man's hands and face were covered in thick, oozing mud. The mud was turning into slime and soaking through his shoes. Field Supervisor Arthur Collins, looking up, red-faced with effort of moving around in a confined space, said, 'Well, it's what's left of a three foot wide water pipe when some lunatic sets a bomb off above it in the middle of the road.' He had a thick Scottish accent of the slow, whimsical brand that got less whimsical when it was someone else doing the whimsy. Collins, wiping his hands on his hastily put on coveralls, said, 'Someone just worked out where the pipe was under the road, shoved some sort of banger exactly along its length on the road above it, and then blew it to pieces.' One of the police photographers from Scientific shoved his way past him in the hole to get a shot of something and trod on his shoes with his mud-encrusted rubber boots, 'The end. Over to you.' The photographer came back and got his muddy rubber boots trodden on by Collins' even muddier shoes. 'Someone told me it was a gang of workmen. Is that right?'

Feiffer put out his hand to help Collins out of the hole. Collins, to his credit, shook his head. Or maybe it was only that, so far, Feiffer hadn't trodden on his shoes. 'Maybe. According to the witnesses such as they are.' He saw Collins' face. 'Sorry about your shoes.'

'Thanks.' Collins, slipping at the rim and coming down on his knees, said with feeling, 'Well, they aren't any of my people. The one thing you can say about the people who work for my department is that the last thing they'd do on their own time – or anyone else's for that matter – is blow up a road in order to give themselves work.' He got himself up and looked down at his feet. 'We have enough trouble getting them to fix roads let alone smash them up.' He looked down at his shoes.

'Do your people usually work at night?'

'They weren't my people. My people, as a matter of fact, those who were leaning on their shovels last night, were leaning on them within haggis-throwing distance of here.' Collins said with bitterness at the state of his shoes, 'A little Scottish humour to disguise that fact that I'm highly annoyed at being got out of my bed to clamber around in holes before breakfast. And before you start asking about trucks, all the Department trucks have been accounted for and are exactly where they should be: either in the compound or at their appointed place of vigorous work with their drivers collapsed over their steering wheels having a good long snooze.' Collins said evenly, 'Chief Inspector, since I, like you, am a public servant all I can say after a long and detailed examination of the events that took place during the night on the roadway of Isandula Street, Hong Bay, is "Sorry, not my department."' He rubbed at a speck of mud in the corner of his eye, 'I'm glad no one was hurt, but as to what the point of it was –'

'How long before you can get the street open to traffic again?'

'Days.' Behind him the photographer took a series of shots and began climbing out of the hole holding his hand out for Collins to help him. Collins took a step away, 'Maybe three or four if I can re-assign a gang; if I can't, then a week.' He saw something yellow in the mud where a helmeted and visored officer from the Bomb Squad was down on his hands and knees probing the mire with a silver rod, 'And no, we don't use yellow plastic ribbons when we cordon off a street, and yes, we do usually work at night because of the traffic, and no, no one reported to my office that there was any work, illegal or otherwise, going on in Isandula Street.' He was thinking of a long, hot bath and clean clothes. 'So over to you.' He asked, 'Someone said there was also a girl in the Mini – is she all right?'

'She's in hospital with a few bruises and shock.' Feiffer, gazing down into the hole, said curiously, 'Look, have you any idea at all why—'

'No.' Collins, shaking his head, said firmly, 'No.' He looked back into the hole where the photographer was still trying to clamber out and reached down to grasp his hands and extract him with a jerk, 'Sorry. Neither I nor the Department can offer you one suggestion – solid or otherwise – why what happened here happened.'

Isandula Street. The name commemorated a town in South Africa that, during the Zulu Wars of the 1870's, had been the scene of the single most shattering defeat in the history of British arms since the Norman Conquest.

Street Of Three Fishermen. Below the English on the street sign the Chinese name was laid out in neatly embossed square formal characters.

7.12 a.m.

In the hole in the middle of the street, you could tell by the silence, no one was finding anything.

It was unfathomable. At the rim of the pit, Feiffer, not knowing quite what he was predicating it on, said softly as Collins began to squelch towards his car to go home to a warm, tranquil, cleansing bath, 'Great.'

7.13 and a half. Almost fifty good, fruitful minutes of shouting, yelling, arm-waving and bonnet-kicking before he had to stand back on the sidewalk and let any car on Earth that wished to drive up and station itself in front of a parking meter for a limited period.

For a limited period. That was the bit that counted.

In General Gordon Street, P.C. Number 69162 Lo said with a happy sigh, 'Ahhh . . .'

He touched at the ticket book in the top pocket of his pressed khaki shirt to check it was still there.

It was. Lo said again, 'Ahhh . . .'

Traffic Evaluation Experiment Penalty For Removal $200
To hell with that. That was someone else's pleasure.

7.14 a.m. The Good Germ, leaping into the honking, hooting, bumper to bumper mess of General Gordon Street, believing with the Uniform that he might live forever, leapt back into happy, abusive action.

He was not going to live forever.

In General Gordon Street as the traffic fought its way unendingly into the increasing brightness of the day, Lo's remaining life span was being counted off, by someone somewhere, in mere, ticking minutes.

2

The Hong Bay Dharma Datu monastery on Hong Bay Beach
Road had been created as an oasis of quiet calm. It had been
created as an oasis of quiet calm so the monks in the Dharma
Datu monastery on Hong Bay Beach Road could turn it into a
raving madhouse. In the incense-filled cedar-floored loft on
the third floor, Detective Inspector Phil Auden, searching for
bullet holes, yelled above the chaos, 'What the hell are they
doing now? It sounds like they're all having mass orgasms in a
bloody echo chamber!'

To say he was searching for bullet holes was putting it
mildly. With the screaming, bell ringing, wind chime tinkling
and assorted cacophony he was hanging like some demented
bat from a lacquered rafter jabbing at the roof tiles with a ball
point pen. Auden shouted down to Detective Inspector Spencer
spread full length above a trap door in the narrow space, 'I
thought bloody Zen Buddhist monks went in for quiet stuff
like meditation and bloody flower growing.' He found a bullet
hole. It was at least .75 calibre. That figured. In madhouses
no one did anything by halves. Auden, twisting into a
position that would have given a contortionist ear-ache,
demanded, 'Well? Aye? What in God's name are they doing
down there?'

Down on the second floor, the monks, shaven headed and
saffron robed, looking from Spencer's angle like dressed eggs,

were hitting each other with bamboo canes. Spencer said, 'They're searching for Enlightenment.'

'With what? Bloody pile drivers?' He could take the thumping and yelling and howling. It was the tinkling of the wind chimes that got to him. Auden, finding another bullet hole and ramming his pen into it to check the angle of trajectory, screamed, 'I thought it was only the bloody Tibetans who went in for all this bell ringing business. These people are Chinese. I thought the Chinese Enlightenment bit went in for bloody calligraphy and quiet.' The bullet had come straight up from the floor of the loft and gone equally straight up into infinity. What had been in its way, a top layer of tiling on the roof, had gone straight down and almost killed an old lady in the monastery garden there to do nothing more shootable-for than let a caged bird out of its cage as an act of merit. Auden shouted, 'What happened to all this "sound of one hand clapping" business Zen people are supposed to go in for?' He shouted, 'I read a book before I came here and it had pictures of people sitting around looking quiet in it!' It had been an old book. Auden, finding another shattered tile (this one had cascaded down onto a cripple), yelled, 'Aye? Well?'

The noise stopped and the monks went straight back to wall gazing. Auden yelled, 'These people are bloody crazy!' In the sudden silence he waited for a reply. He knew Spencer also read books about things like Zen. Spencer bought his books new. Auden, twisting back on the rafter to hang upside down like some sort of monstrous, fawn-suited Cheshire cat wearing a holstered Colt Python, said as one reader to another, 'Isn't that right, Bill? Zen is supposed to be very quiet. Isn't it?' The last line in the book had said there wasn't very much to Zen. Since the author had taken almost sixty pages to get to that conclusion it could either have been the final thought or just a function of him getting pissed off at page fifty-nine. Auden, trying to be tolerant where things like religion were concerned, said mildly, still upside down, 'There isn't much to Zen, you know.'

There wasn't much to fifteen bullet holes in the tiled roof

either, least of all a reason why, over the last three days, someone had taken the trouble to put them there.

Auden said, 'On the thousand year old bronze temple bell a butterfly sits resting.' He waited for a reaction.

Spencer said, 'Hmm.'

Auden had made notes from the book. One thing it wasn't going to be in a Zen Buddhist monastery was ignoramus week. Auden said, 'Empty handed I go/And yet, a spade is in my hand/I walk on foot/And yet, I ride on the back of an ox/When I cross the river the bridge flows/And the water –' Auden said softly raising one finger (it was about all that was holding him up) '– and the water is still.' He wasn't any sort of ignoramus. He had read a book. Auden, hanging on for dear life, said with a strange clenched teeth fixed grin, 'Well, what do you make of all that?'

Spencer said, 'They're all novices down there. They're new at all this. You can tell by their recently shaved heads. Their Master is still in China. They probably don't know much more about Zen than we do.'

Well, you couldn't expect to impress people overnight. Auden, jabbing his free foot into a niche and hauling his two hundred pound six foot two inch bulk up into a section of rafter built to hold a one ounce eight inch long incense stick, said as his master stroke, 'There-really-isn't-much-to-Zen-at-all.'

There wasn't much to his handhold either. He was going. His finger was slipping off the rafter and he was going. Auden, never one to give in easily, said, 'Right, Bill? Right?' Lately, as he felt himself getting older, he thought he needed a few friends. He was starting off with Spencer. To get friendship you had to be friendly. You had to take an interest. Auden said, 'Too true, aye?' He felt himself going. Auden said quickly, 'Well, that's the universe covered. Now how about the little question of who shot the bullet holes in the monastery roof.' He was beginning to make little panting noises as his body realized it was about to crash down onto a fragile cedarwood floor, pass one storey down onto another fragile cedarwood floor and then, crashing through that and possibly another cedarwood floor, find itself travelling at terminal velocity in the general direction of a far from fragile cement basement. Auden said, 'Right, Bill? Right . . . ?' Auden said suddenly as everything including him on the rafter went in a creaking of rotten timber and crack of equally rotten joists, '*Aahhh!*'

Up and out of the mire of ignorance into the light of knowledge, power and friendship.

Auden, his ankle, his leg, his arm, his spine and his spirit hurting like they were each of them broken in no less than eighteen places, said with happy, friendly expectation in his heart, 'Right, Bill? *Right?*'

'Put a coin in.' In General Gordon Street, Lo, tapping his wristwatch, yelled above the chaos of the traffic, 'Put a coin in!' It was 8.01. Time to feed the meters. Lo, wedging himself in hard between the first meter in the long line and a table top truck taking up two spaces, stuck his head in through the open passenger side window and ordered, 'Put a coin in the other meter too. You're taking up two spaces so you put two coins in!' Down the line the cars were coming in like hungry vultures. Lo, giving the rusty door of the truck a wallop with his fist that brought down a cascade of corrosion, shouted, 'Don't you make yourself comfortable in there! Two spaces equals two coins!'

The driver was one of those short, bald, cement-brained people who thought he could go through life protected by his own stupidity. The driver, gazing at him and shrugging, gave him an angelic smile. The driver, looking innocent, said in Cantonese, 'I don't speak Cantonese.'

Lo, gritting his teeth, said in Mandarin, 'You're taking up two spaces so you have to put in two coins.' He reached into his pocket and held up a fifty cent coin, 'Two! Two coins for two meters!' All down the line of the other thirty meters people were putting their money in. Lo yelled, '*Put another coin in!*'

The driver smiled at him. His load on the back of the table

top was boxes of plastic dolls' heads. People who dealt with children thought they could get away with anything. Lo, reaching into his top pocket for his ticket book with one hand and making little pantomime insertions of his fifty cent coin into the meter with the other, said menacingly, 'Look, coin. Meter. Two spaces. Got it? Three seconds and then –' The meter gulped his coin. Lo said, 'Right! That does it! Now you're going for non compliance with the traffic laws *and* theft by deception from a police officer!' Lo, considering for the briefest moment doing a Dirty Harry and using his .38 to blow the driver out of his cab and into the next world, ordered, 'Get out of the truck! *Now!* Get out of the truck!'

Behind him he heard a strange sound, a click. Lo, turning around to look as the driver began to lever himself out of the cab still looking stupid, said in total exasperation, 'Now the meter's broken! It's all your fault! It's your duty to report broken meters and now it's –' It had been the strangest sound. It had come from inside the meter. Lo said, 'I'm going to run you in for everything I can think of and then, when I get my book of regulations, a few things no one has ever thought of!' There was a thin wire running down the side of the meter, going to the hose. Lo said, 'I'm going to –'

He looked down the line of meters and then to the traffic experiment hose that ran along the ground the full length of them, resting against their stanchions. There was a wire from the hose into the first meter. Lo said –

He heard a click.

Forgetting momentarily about the driver, but with his hand still on his pocket where the tickets were, P.C. Number 69162 Lo bent down to put his ear against the side of the meter to listen.

In the loft, Detective Inspector Spencer was working out The Nature Of Things. He was working out whether the bullet holes in the roof were bullet holes at all.

Maybe, according to Auden's book, where it said you should never take any empirical phenomenon in the world at face value, he was even working out whether the roof was a roof at all.

To get a friend you had to be a friend.

Auden said, 'Well?'

He waited, rubbing at his ankle.

Spencer said thoughtfully, 'Hmm . . .'

Against the row of meters, against his ankles, the hose jumped as if a surge of electrical power ran briefly through it and then, finding a way out, was discharged into the air. In General Gordon Street, forgetting for a moment the dolls' heads driver and his fifty cents, P.C. Number 69162 Lo got down on his hands and knees to examine it.

It felt warm.

He picked the hose up in his hand and tested its weight.

It felt heavy.

He peered hard at it for official markings.

There might have been sermons in stone, but in explosives there was poetry. In the Isandula Street blast there had been an entire Epithalamion. In the Bomb Squad laboratory of the Scientific Branch on Aberdeen Street, Technical Inspector Matthews, picking up the total remains from almost two hours digging in the crater, on the Mini and up and down the street for fifty yards, said with admiration, 'Beautiful. A joy to behold.' The total remains were two scorched and tattered plastic ribbons the bombers had used to make their cordon and six bags containing what looked like about forty pounds of thick, slimy mud waiting to give up its secrets. The only secrets the mud was going to give up was that it was mud. Matthews said softly, 'Perfect. The perfect, ideal, cut to the bone, no frills, do exactly what it's supposed to blasting job.' He picked up one of the plastic bags of mud and discarded it again as nothing more than a bag full of mud. 'This is what people mean when they talk about blowing things up. Whoever did this did just that: he blew everything *up*.' He smiled. He had the dirtiest hands in the world. He said with admiration,

'They wanted it. They planned it, they laid it, and they did it.'

Feiffer said, 'Did what?' The entire room was lined with hymns to the joy of the Big Bang theory ranging from collections of hand grenades to collections of photographs of what hand grenades did. 'What did they do? What they did was blow up a water pipe.' It wasn't dirt on the man's hands or on his coveralls, it was dried in explosives. Feiffer said, irritated, 'I'm glad you think it was such a wonderful, slap up example of the gentle art of –'

'It is.' Matthews, gazing longingly at a technical drawing of a German DM 51 grenade fitted with a fragmentation sleeve and then at another drawing showing little match men being blown to pieces within a radius of ten yards from where the fragmentation sleeve had fragmented, said with feeling, 'That's what you don't understand. That's what nobody understands. It *is* a gentle art. The gentle art of blowing something up consists in blowing something up – nothing else, just what you want to blow up. And that's what they did.' He touched at one of the bags of mud and gave it a pat. 'What they used here wasn't some sort of coarse bloody gunpowder, you know. What they used here was a very highly sophisticated, hand made form of *plastique* moulded into shaped charges and set off at just the right angle to do the job.' He stopped patting the mud and gave it a contemptuous slap, 'See this? It's mud. It's garbage. It isn't bits and pieces of unburnt powder or lumps of bloody casing and bits and pieces of old alarm clocks and wire, what it is is mud.' He had a slightly mad look in his eye. Maybe it came with the territory. 'What these guys wanted they got. What they wanted was a water pipe and' – he gazed at the grenade picture – 'and when you want something and you're bright and you understand explosives you go out and you make something like this.'

'*Like what?*'

'Like half a dozen paint tins filled with shaped cutting charges and a high flash detonator to set it off at just the right velocity.' No one understood. 'Don't you see what they've done? They've actually cut through six feet of solid bitumen and chopped up a cement water pipe without' – he tapped his finger against the mud. The mud made a slurping noise. '– without sending one single blast wave upwards. Not one.' He sighed with admiration. 'They set up no less than about thirty pounds of probably the highest potency stuff you can make on your kitchen table without moving into the realms of popping out to buy plutonium and they set it off without even ruffling one single brick on any of the buildings in the entire street and without breaking one single window.' He said, shaking his head, 'Wonderful. I only know one other person in the entire Colony who could have done it and that's me and even I'm not sure.' He looked at his hands. 'I might try it out on the Police Bomb Range at the weekend.'

'They almost killed two people in a car!'

'Did they? Did they?' Matthews, consumed with delight at the pure professionalism of it, said, still shaking his head, 'No. If they'd wanted to kill two people in a car then two people in a car would have been killed. What they did was set out to blow up a water pipe and that was what they did. The mud and the water almost killed the two people in the car.' He looked annoyed. 'What the hell were they doing there anyway? It must have been almost pitch black at that time of morning. The guys in the street had a cordon up. If those two had got killed it would have been their own fault.' The laboratory was in a steel-lined room in the basement. You could see why. Matthews said, 'You want to know why they did it, don't you?' He gave Feiffer no chance to answer. He gazed at the drawing of the grenade. 'You don't understand anything about this level of things, do you?' He smiled. Even his teeth were explosive stained and, where he had spent a lifetime crimping primers, chipped and broken. 'You want to know, don't you? Well, I can tell you. They did it – they blew up a water pipe in a deserted street – not people, not buildings, not anything, not anything important, but just an underground water pipe – just about the most difficult thing you could do with explosives – they did it because it was there.' He was

31

raving. His eyes were glittering. Matthews said, 'I'm an artist. I know another artist's work. And that's what this is: it's art.'

'*Are you trying to tell me that whoever did this did it just to see if he could do it?*' It was another world. He had crossed over. Feiffer said, '*Are you completely out of your mind?*'

There was no clock inside the basement laboratory of the Scientific Branch.

There was no need.

In there, it was always, forever, night.

About this time The Old Auden would have said something obnoxious. That was the reason The Old Auden didn't have any friends. The New Auden didn't say anything. The New Auden waited. It was a trial. In the loft of the Dharma Datu monastery on Hong Bay Beach Road, The New Auden watching The Old Spencer contemplating, simply said, 'Carry on.'

The New Auden understood. His friend Spencer was walking up and down thinking about the nature of things, being an intellectual. As you got older you felt a need to have a few intellectual friends. *Guns and Ammo* didn't reach the Colony until the first week in the next month, and by the third week, you were looking for someone to talk to. In the loft, Auden, setting a grin to his face and, with Spencer, gazing up at the roof (or was it the non-roof? The New Auden was prepared to consider anything), said again, 'Carry on.'

At this point in the proceedings, The Old Auden would have pointed out that a .75 calibre bullet hole in a roof was a .75 calibre bullet hole in a roof. The New Auden said quietly, 'Well, fascinating, isn't it?' He had a funny, tight feeling in his stomach. It was called patience. The New Auden said, 'Well, gosh, it's really worth working things out right from the beginning. That way we won't make any errors we'll regret later.' The feeling in his stomach turned into positive nausea. One thing at a time. After this, Spencer could be nice to him. Auden said —

Spencer, as was his right as a separate individual, as a person of worth, as someone to be considered on his own terms, in

32

his own time, on his own level, as a friend, said vaguely, 'Hmm . . .' He was still striding up and down trying to work out whether the bullet holes were bullet holes at all.

Auden said gently, 'Take your time.' He almost said, 'Old man.' '. . . no hurry at all.' His ankle hurt. He was winning. He was making a friend. The Old Auden, on the other hand . . . The New Auden said thoughtfully, 'You know, Bill, I think they are bullet holes actually . . .' The New Auden said . . .

He saw a trapdoor open in the far corner of the room. He saw, just for an instant, something dark green, bronze, poke its snout up. He saw, just for a fraction, what looked like a burning incense taper. He saw . . .

He saw the muzzle of a Chinese hand cannon.

The Old Auden, taking The New Auden by the throat and throttling him at birth the way he should have done hours ago, leaping at the wandering bloody idiot in the loft and knocking him to the floor, yelled at the top of his voice as the blast from the gun shook every beam and rafter in the place and filled the loft with smoke, 'You stupid, bloody fucking idiot! Bloody goddamned lousy books! Why the hell aren't you bloody *normal*?!'

They were all coming down. One by one, in an instant, they were all being blasted out of the ground by the hose and all the meters in the street were coming down. They were falling like sunflowers, disappearing in smoke and flame as the hose jerked and exploded and tore them off at their bases one by one. He saw it happening. He heard it. Through the sidewalk, on his knees at the far meter, P.C. Lo felt the blasts as, one by one, in his street, all the fine, new parking meters, one by one, serially, were sliced through and turned into junk. He saw them fall. He saw their glass shatter and their metal and paint coming off. They were being hacked down, chopped, destroyed. It was going: his street. His entire street was being changed and destroyed and turned into something else. He saw people running.

His street was being destroyed. P.C. Lo shrieked, '*No.*'

33

He was holding the jumping, burning hose in his hands. He tried to think of where to put it to stop it. There was nowhere. There was no way to stop it. It was coming, reaching for him: the meters were falling one by one. He was at the last meter in the row. There was nothing, nowhere. He had nothing but his uniform. It was everything he had ever had or wanted to have. In the street, his entire body shaking with the effort of holding the living, jerking, lethal hose up off the ground, P.C. Lo, at the end of everything that had ever meant anything to him, yelled with his face turned upwards in awful, useless, terrible supplication to anyone who might listen, 'No. Oh, no.'

P.C. Lo yelled, 'Please! Please! *Please help me stop it!*'

3

On the phone in the Detectives' Room O'Yee said in exasperation, 'What do you mean, "What does it do?" It's a *dog*.'

The last potential dog owner had been a cop at the North
Point Station who had a share in a restaurant. He had asked
what weight it dressed out at. O'Yee said, 'It's a dog. It's a
standard, run-of-the-mill, ordinary, see them everywhere goddamned dog!' The trouble was that in Hong Kong, the world's
greatest paean of praise to the petless high rise apartment, you
didn't see them everywhere. 'Mutt. Hound. Man's best friend.
Canis familiaris!' He had looked it up in the Station encyclo-
paedia, but the Boy's Book Of Knowledge for 1907 was
singularly unhelpful about the placement of dog meat – 'How
the hell do I know what it dresses out at? I've never owned a
goddamned dog before, have I?' O'Yee said desperately, 'Well,
do you at least know someone who might know someone who
might want a dog?' It was a great dog: no trouble at all. Put it
on a filthy linoleum floor and it covered three or four square
feet of the filth without a murmur. O'Yee said a moment
before he hung up, 'You people over there, what do you do
with your stray dogs?' O'Yee said, 'Forget it.'

He looked down at the dog. Somewhere, there had to be
someone with a kind, understanding nature, someone who,
when faced with the dregs of this world, felt a stab in his heart
of understanding, a forgiving, good, simple soul with a love of

his fellow man and Christian fellowship abounding: someone who could not resist a dog.

Hong Kong was a big town.

It wasn't that big.

O'Yee said softly, 'God.'

He tried urgently to think of what to do.

He didn't want to look in. Lo was inside there, on a bunk in the ambulance with Detective Chief Inspector Feiffer leaning over him, and whatever else he wanted to do what he didn't want to do was look in. In General Gordon Street, the traffic was flowing again around the cordoned off side of the street where the meters had been and there was noise and chaos, but he couldn't hear it. In there, in the back of the ambulance Lo was lying half covered by a sheet, ashen faced, and all he could hear was the sound of the plasma dripping through the tubes into his arm as, bit by bit, all the life ebbed away from him. At the back of the ambulance, Chief Inspector Kyle-Foxby, touching at the brightly polished brass button on his shirt pocket where in his branch, Traffic, that most important of all items, the ticket book, was kept, said softly, 'Matthews, isn't it?'

By him, still in his coveralls, Matthews, looking down at the piece of charred and burned hosepipe in his hand, said quietly, 'Yes, sir.' Kyle-Foxby was no more than twenty-two years old with a soft, bright young man's face. Matthews said evenly, 'Technical Branch. Explosives.' He had also never seen anyone dying before. He glanced in and saw Feiffer's eyes flick over to him. Matthews said, 'Thermite with a high velocity spreading charge. The sort of stuff used to cut through railway lines. Home made.' He lowered the hose and glanced at Kyle-Foxby trying to understand. Matthews said, 'That must be interesting, sir, your department.' He saw Feiffer bend down to touch at something on Lo's chest, leaning down as if to listen and he asked quickly, 'Can I help?' He saw Feiffer look back to him and shake his head. 'Um, they say that for a young man Traffic is probably the most –' He lost track of what he was going to say. Matthews, looking into the ambulance as Feiffer rested his

36

hand gently on Lo's shoulder, said, rubbing at his head, 'Thermite. It's the stuff you use to cut straight through railway lines. It's —' But Lo's hands were in a box at the end of the ambulance floor. Matthews said suddenly, 'The poor bastard must have picked up the hose and held it when it went off.'

In the street the traffic was flowing again and you would have thought there would have been nothing to hear except that traffic.

All Kyle-Foxby could hear was the steady dripping of the plasma.

In the ambulance, Feiffer, leaning down with his hand still on Lo's shoulder, said softly in Chinese, 'Lo, it's Chief Inspector Feiffer from Yellowthread Street. Do you know what happened?' There was blood seeping through the two bandaged stumps on top of the sheet that covered him. Feiffer, patting the man gently on the shoulder and looking at his eyes for comprehension, said softly, 'Lo, you know me. We worked together once or twice before you transferred to Traffic. Did you see anyone or —' He bent down to listen to the man's laboured breathing. It was 8.24. In his cab, the ambulanceman was waiting patiently so he could go directly to the Morgue instead of having to go through the formalities of having Lo declared dead on arrival at St Paul's hospital eight blocks away. He was not going to have to wait long. Feiffer, shaking the grey faced man harder on the shoulder, said firmly, 'It's your duty to tell me what happened.'

In the street, Kyle-Foxby, looking down at the burned hose, said abruptly, 'What did you say?' It was the most important field of police work a young man could get into. Since 1903 when the New York police commissioner had framed the first Rules For Drivers and formed the first Traffic Squad, it had been the one single most important aspect of police work. Kyle-Foxby, swallowing, said, 'I've got a degree, you see. That's why I've got the rank.' He looked around. 'Hong Kong is sudden death for an English cop really — I mean, it really, totally marks you as some sort of lunatic dreamer who thinks wasting five years out in the mysterious East is the way to get

37

ahead, but in Traffic it's a godsend.' He looked at Matthews and saw how dirty the man was, 'Hong Kong has the worst traffic congestion in the world and if you can get in a few years' experience out here, then it's a different matter –' In the ambulance there was a strange, sighing noise. It was coming from Lo's chest. 'In Hong Kong you can get more experience dealing with chaos than almost anywhere in the –' Inside the ambulance, Lo's life was ending and there was nothing anyone could do about it. He heard Feiffer say urgently, 'Lo. Lo. Can you hear me?' 'It must be about the only place on Earth that –' Kyle-Foxby said suddenly, 'Jesus Christ, this is ridiculous! What's the point of it?' On the other side of the cordon the traffic was moving the way it was supposed to do. All that had happened was that a few parking meters had been cut down. There were plenty of spare parking meters. In two or three days they would all be back in place. Kyle-Foxby, staring at the dirt and muck on Matthews' coveralls and on his hands, said, shaking his head, 'People aren't supposed to get hurt in this department. The worst that should happen is that they'll get involved in a dispute with a motorist.' He looked at the hose. 'What the hell's thermite got to do with that?'

It was Hong Bay. It was the district his people had to work in. For an instant, as he leaned forward over the bunk, he saw the butt of Feiffer's .38 Detective Special clipped by a worn strap in his belt holster. Kyle-Foxby said shaking his head, 'This is crazy! That business on Isandula Street was crazy, but I thought it was someone after a bank or something and that it concerned people like you and –' He jerked his thumb, not in the direction of Feiffer, but in the direction of Feiffer's gun – 'And him. People who – people who –' Kyle-Foxby said, 'Garbage! People like him and you who deal all your lives with garbage!' In the ambulance one of his men was dying. He heard the breathing become rapid. Kyle-Foxby said, 'I spent years at university getting a degree in urban planning so I could come to this job – no, not this job, but a decent job – in the Police with full, professional qualifications, I didn't come to –' Kyle-Foxby said, 'This is cops and robbers stuff!' He was twenty-two years old. 'It shouldn't be anything I have to take part in or any of my people should have to take part in, it should be –'

'Lo. Can you hear me? *Lo*.'

In the cab of the ambulance, the ambulance driver, in no hurry, was lighting a cigarette.

Feiffer said urgently, 'Lo, listen to me. It's important you help me before anyone else gets hurt.' He was losing. The only sound in the ambulance was the steady dripping of the plasma. Feiffer, pushing harder on the man's shoulder, said desperately in Cantonese, 'Lo, please . . . please help us.'

He needed a cigarette. He didn't smoke, but he needed something to do with his hands. In the street, Chief Inspector Kyle-Foxby, trying to look away, said, 'God damn it!' He looked at the hose in Matthews' hand. Scorched and burned, it looked like some awful hangman's rope. Kyle-Foxby said, 'This isn't right.' He looked out at the traffic and saw only blurs. 'The whole point of this sort of police work is to create a well balanced healthy system like – like a body.' That was how he put it to his policemen. It was a bloodstream. They were Good Germs in a healthy, functioning body. Kyle-Foxby said, 'It isn't right that someone did this. It disrupts everything.' He was rubbing at his hand. In the early Autumn weather he was sweating. He touched at the button of his khaki shirt and felt the wetness of perspiration starting under his arm. Kyle-Foxby said, '*What the hell did anyone do this for?*' He saw Feiffer come out of the ambulance with blood on his hand. (For a moment he saw the ugly little gun again on his belt as his suit coat came open.) Kyle-Foxby, trying to understand, said, 'Is he dead? Is he dead yet?' He saw Feiffer's face.

At the front of the ambulance, the driver, a stocky middle-aged Chinese wearing a short white coat, got out of his cab to come round.

Kyle-Foxby, looking first to Feiffer and then to Matthews still holding the hose in his hands, asked, 'Well?'

He saw Feiffer's face.

All around him, in General Gordon Street, the traffic was

flowing in a planned, orderly, controlled manner. He saw Feiffer pause at the steps of the ambulance and light a cigarette.

There was nothing to say.

All any of them had heard for the nineteen minutes it had taken Lo to die was the sound of the plasma.

In the street, all the creases in his uniform going with the rising heat of the day, touching at his buttons, Chief Inspector Kyle-Foxby, aged twenty-two, said in the terrible silence as, inside the ambulance, the ambulanceman turned off the drip, 'Please, somebody – *what in God's name is going on?*'

It was a man in a grey business suit. One of the wall-gazers had seen him as he ran past the open door to the monastery corridor. In the corridor, Auden, kicking down cell doors as fast as his size 10 shoes could kick, yelled to Spencer on the other side of the corridor also kicking, 'Chinese, about five seven, full head of hair, carrying something shiny in his hand!' The something shiny was a .75 calibre antique Chinese single-shot bronze hand cannon which once you worked up the nerve to fire, would take the head off whatever you were firing at as if it had never been there in the first place. Auden, splintering wood and sweeping the room with his .357 magnum before moving on to the next, yelled, 'If you see him, don't fuck around. He's had time to reload it.' You had to set the thing off at the touch hole with a taper. There was no shortage of tapers. The rooms and the corridors were all full of burning incense sticks. Auden, tensing himself at the door to the next cell, yelled, 'If you see him, shoot him.' He kicked the door in and dived into the room with his gun out in front of him.

Across from him, Spencer yelled, 'Nothing.' They were going down the rooms one by one. There were only two left. Spencer, putting his shoulder to a particularly heavy piece of camphorwood separating yet another monk's cell from the reality of the world, yelled, 'Not in here. Only one left on this side.' There was another crash as he took out the last door. 'Nothing. He isn't in any of these rooms.'

There was only one door left on Auden's side. Auden,

kicking at it, ready to kill, yelled, 'Nothing here either.' Wherever the shooter had gone, he had gone completely. Maybe he had never existed. Maybe – Maybe the place was getting to him. Auden, holstering his gun, said, 'Maybe those bloody monks are lying to us. Maybe –' He heard a sound. He looked up. Above him the cedarwood ceiling, like the rest of the monastery brought piece by piece from China, was dropping little spumes of dust.

Auden said, 'Dammit, he's up there.' He heard a sound: a match being struck or a – Auden yelled, 'Get down. He's above us and he's going to –' He actually heard the fizz as the powder in the touchhole caught and the flame went speeding down the main charge in the – He actually heard the ignition. He actually heard – He heard a terrible, shattering blast that brought dust and splinters of wood down onto his head. He heard bits and pieces of material fly about. He actually heard the bullet as if –

No, he didn't. It didn't come. It was going the other way. On the floor, holding Spencer's head down yet again, Auden clearly heard the shooter, armed with his antique bronze hand cannon, shoot yet another harmless hole in the roof.

He heard, as a scrabbling, the shooter run away, safe, out of reach.

He heard, outside in the garden, the sound of someone yell as smashed and broken tiles cascaded down on his head.

He heard Spencer, suffocating under his hand, say, 'Huh! Huh!'

It was insane, mad, lunatic.

Up there, running fast, in the crawl space, he heard someone, very softly, start to giggle.

In the public phone at the corner of General Gordon and Soochow Streets, Feiffer said for the second time, 'I don't know, Neal. I don't know what it's supposed to prove because so far, to date, all it's proved is that they can blow up underground water pipes and chop down bloody parking meters.' On the Commander's end of the line there was a silence. In the street, the Traffic and the Department Of Main Roads people were out in force collecting the cut down parking meters and loading them into vans. 'According to Inspector Matthews of Scientific whoever's doing it is some sort of explosives genius we've about as much chance of catching in the act or picking up from physical evidence as the Japanese had of cracking the Manhattan Project.' The Traffic and Main Roads people were keeping well away from the last cut down meter in the row because of the blood on the footpath. 'They're actually making the stuff: shaped cutting charges set off by radio control and thermite set off by the clockwork inside parking meters.' If you had that sort of mind, a city was one enormous playground. 'If they put their minds to it there's probably no limit to what they can do.'

'How many of them are there?'

'At least four or five of them. The only sighting we have is from Isandula Street and according to The Embarrassment Man who's half blind anyway there seemed to be at least that many of them at the cordon wearing dust masks.'

'And at the meters?'

'And at the meters, nothing.' In traditional police work, where people had the consideration to kill, maim or blow each other up inside houses you could knock on doors until you found someone who had seen or heard something. Feiffer, glancing at the traffic increasing serially and at the total concentration on the drivers' faces as they got on with the business of just staying alive on the road, said, 'Less than nothing.' Even Hong Kong Chinese, the world's greatest spectators, called it a day and put their foot on the gas when the street started blowing up around them. Feiffer said again, 'Nothing. We've got nothing at all.'

'What's your next move?'

'Other than the usual useless appeals for witnesses, I haven't got a next move.'

'You said Lo lived for a good fifteen minutes in the ambulance. He must have said *something* –'

'No.' What he had said had had nothing to do with the

bombs. What he had said was, 'Help me.' He had had both his hands burned off at the wrists and by the time the ambulance had arrived he had lost over three pints of blood. It was still there on the fallen meter and in the gutter. Feiffer said, 'No, he didn't say anything.'

'There's no possibility that it was Lo they were after? And in Isandula Street —'

'What? Two lovers in a car who happened to turn up on the off-chance and an Embarrassment Man who turned up because the lovers turned up?' The Main Roads people had got to the blood. One of them called to his field director, Arthur Collins, and Collins, motioning to Chief Inspector Kyle-Foxby went reluctantly to the area to see what could be done. Feiffer said, 'No. What they did was what they did: they blew up an underground water pipe that, in fact, isn't used for anything more important than bleeding off the excess from the area for recycling and then they took out thirty parking meters that aren't used for anything more important than keeping a clearway clear in the rush hour.' It didn't make any sense at all. Feiffer, echoing Inspector Matthews, said, 'I have the strongest feeling that killing Lo was an accident and so was any damage they might have done to anyone in Isandula Street.'

'Crime isn't an accident.' In his office in Kowloon overlooking the harbour, the Commander said with rising irritation, 'You talk as if it's just a gang of little boys playing with firecrackers.' He also had superiors to explain it to. 'Little boys with firecrackers don't go around lifting half a bloody street out of its foundations and taking people's hands off at the wrists!' The Commander said tightly, 'A man is dead and it's up to you, Harry, to find out why.'

'I am trying to find out why. So far what I've found out, I've told you.'

'What you've told me so far is nothing. Matthews' report seems to suggest between the lines that it's some sort of *game*. People don't use bloody explosives for games — What are there — five of them? Have you any idea just how unlikely it is that there could be five equally demented bloody little lunatics

43

working together whose idea of a good time is crimping detonators with their teeth and playing around with unstable, home made explosives? Have you any idea just how unlikely it is that someone who knows how to make hand-made high explosives – a craftsman – would go around just blowing things up for the fun of it?'

At the meter, Kyle-Foxby was looking down at the blood. Feiffer, shouting, said, 'No, I don't. *Do you?*'

'What the hell are these bloody people doing? What the hell are they after?'

'*I don't know.*' It was hopeless. It was nothing, a random event – two of them. Feiffer, increasingly frustrated, said tightly into the phone, 'Neal, don't you think the first thing I did was look for a bloody bank tunnelling operation in Isandula Street? There isn't even a bank. And here, don't you think the first thing that occurred to me was that it was an effort to stop a bloody armoured car or something so it could be knocked over? Armoured cars don't use this street, because, like Isandula Street, there isn't anything in General Gordon Street or anywhere around it worth putting into an armoured car! And if it was a rehearsal to stop a vehicle in the street for a kidnapping or an assassination they couldn't have done a worse job if they'd tried. If anything, with the parking meters gone the traffic is flowing faster.' It was hopeless. Feiffer, drawing a breath, said, 'It's only half past eight in the morning and, after having seen two examples of their work, all I can tell is that if the final outcome of this is an atomic bombing of bloody Hong Kong, then, by God, we seem to have found the people who might be able to do it.' Kyle-Foxby and Arthur Collins were still standing looking down at the blood. It seemed to be beyond anyone's wit to get a hose to sluice it away. 'So if you want to know what I'm doing to stop it the answer quite frankly is – *nothing* – because I haven't even got the faintest inkling of an idea what the hell's even supposed to be happening.' Feiffer, turning away from the sight of Collins and Kyle-Foxby looking down, said, shaking, 'What the hell's their next trick? You tell me. The bloody Pentagon? Or have they had enough, proved whatever point it is they're trying to prove, and gone off happily about their normal business?' Feiffer said with heavy irony, 'What is their normal business – booby trap consultants to the bloody Special Forces? I've checked and there's no one with this sort of legal explosive expertise in the Colony except Technical Inspector bloody Matthews himself. And he agrees.' It was hopeless. Feiffer said suddenly, quietly, 'Neal, Lo was an accident but I have a feeling that if this goes on there are going to be a lot more accidents just like it.'

'Is it going to go on?'

'Are you asking for a professional opinion?' At the chopped down meter, gazing down at the pavement, Chief Inspector Kyle-Foxby looked as if he was going to throw up.

'Yes.'

It was 8.37 a.m. on a warm, balmy day. Except for the cordon along the sidewalk and out a few feet into the road, except for the vans and the police cars and the personnel – except for the blood and whatever else was down there on the meter and in the gutter – you could hardly tell anything had happened in the street at all. Nothing stopped the eternal Hong Kong traffic. Louder and louder, as he watched from the phone, it seemed to be roaring in his ears.

It was 8.37 a.m. on a warm, balmy day. On the phone receiver Feiffer's hand was wet with perspiration.

Feiffer, with a sick feeling in his stomach, as at the meter the Mains Roads people went to get buckets of water and brooms from their vans, said quietly, hopelessly, 'Yes, there are going to be more.'

Feiffer said softly, in almost a whisper, watching the street, 'And I don't think unless they make a very big mistake that there's going to be anything anyone can do to stop it.'

8.37 a.m. In Sepoy Street, linking Empress Of India and Khartoum Streets, there was a man having his ears cleaned out by an Ear Wax Man at a roadside stall. It was his left ear mainly. He had had to put up with several very loud noises recently and the wax, pushed hard against his eardrums by the concussion, was becoming painful.

Seated on a wooden stool, he cocked his head up so The Ear Wax Man, a tall, scarecrow-like ragged Chinese, could work more effectively at it with his little ebony handled scrapers and spoons. Sepoy Street, as the morning progressed, was becoming busy with people on their way to work. With only casual glances, they stepped around him and The Ear Wax Man's stool without stopping.

The man having his ears cleaned looked at his watch. His time was limited.

8.38. Nodding and paying the man the few cents the operation had cost, the man stood up and shook his head.

His ears felt better. The pressure was gone. There was a stout, middle-aged woman in black peasant's pyjamas a little down the road selling copies of the morning newspapers: for English readers *The South China Morning Post* and the *Hong Kong Standard* and, for the Chinese-speaker, a full spectrum of all the news and views from Taipei to Peking.

Unhurriedly, he began walking towards Empress Of India Street and, joining the crowd, becoming part of it, became, to his quiet satisfaction, no one special.

He had a small white linen dust mask in the pocket of his coat. Stupidly, he had kept it from the morning's work at Isandula Street as a souvenir.

Sensibly, he dropped it into a trash basket on the sidewalk and, still smiling to himself, kept pace with the moving crowd.

His ears felt better, clearer.

8.39 and a half.

He had slightly less than thirty one minutes to clear the area.

At the corner of the street, glancing constantly at his watch, the man of limited time hailed a taxi.

4

In the Detectives' Room, O'Yee asked, 'Anything?' He saw
Feiffer go to his desk with the preliminary sheaf of Polaroid
photos from Scientific and take out his notebook to start an
organized file. He saw Feiffer, for a moment, put his hand to
his eyes. There was no need to ask. There was nothing. O'Yee
said quietly, 'This Constable Lo, was he the one who worked
here with us with uniformed for a while?'

The file was nothing more than a grey manilla file with a
number on it. Inside it, Lo was going to be nothing more than a
report with yet another number on it. Feiffer, putting his
notebook to one side for a moment and running his hand
across his eyes again, said quietly, 'Yes.' He was also the one
who had had high hopes of a long and successful life. Feiffer
said, 'Constable Lee knows his family. He volunteered to be
the one to tell them.' There was a street map on the wall to one
side of his desk showing the network of roads and lanes and
alleys that made up Hong Bay. It was like one of those mazes in
children's puzzle books which, if you were patient enough, you
could work your way out of with a pencil. In the real maze,
whether you were careful or not, sometimes you ended up
dead in an ambulance with both your hands in a box beside
you.

Feiffer said quietly, 'It was a traffic evaluation experiment.
At least that's what Scientific thinks the sign on the hose said.'

He glanced down at the numbered report that was now P.C. Number 69162 Lo. 'Chief Inspector Kyle-Foxby is under the impression that no one in his right mind could have been taken in by it since it wasn't serial numbered and bloody Vatican censored, but just hand lettered, but poor old Lo, maybe not being quite as clever as bloody Kyle-Foxby —' It was useless. He was wasting his anger. Feiffer said suddenly with his hand to his eyes as if he was trying to rub something away, 'Christopher, these buggers seem to be winning all the time.'

'Winning what? What are they trying to do?'

'I don't know what they're trying to do. For all I know, they're not trying to do anything.' He glanced at the map. In the intricate web Isandula Street was the smallest of parallel lines, General Gordon Street only marginally bigger. In the giant criss-cross of Hong Bay — let alone Hong Kong itself — they represented nothing more than a few squiggles. They represented nothing. There were prime crime targets marked on the map: armoured car firms and banks and large pay roll factories, but neither of the streets was anywhere near any of them. 'For all I know —' Feiffer, seeing the dog asleep on the floor, said abruptly, 'What the hell's that?'

'It's a dog.' O'Yee, staring at the map to keep Feiffer's attention, said defensively, 'I'm trying to find out who owns it.'

'Oh.' In the final analysis, when you looked at it hard enough you realized that no map ever went anywhere. All it did was come back to the same place it started from. Feiffer, shaking his head, said without looking at the dog, 'Send it to the pound.'

'I don't want to send it to the pound.'

Isandula Street, General Gordon Street: they both commemorated defeats. Around them were other streets: Soochow, Empress Of India, Sepoy Street, Generalissimo Chen Street. Feiffer, forgetting the dog for a moment, said absently, 'Where do these names come from? Who makes them up?' He glanced down at the sleeping animal for a second, 'What sort of dog is it? I mean, is it owned by Europeans or Chinese or Malays or what?'

'How the hell do I know?'

Another of the streets was named Moore's Pocket. That was only in English. In Chinese, the name of the street was the Street Of The American Dragon. Feiffer said irritably, 'You know because you ask the bloody thing in a language it understands.' He looked down at the dog and tugged it gently on the ear to wake it. Feiffer, still glancing back and forth to the map, said roughly, '*Aiy-gou! Lai! Wu-fan! Lai! Xian-zai!*' He got no reaction. '*Anjung, makanan!*' He said, shaking his head, 'Well, it isn't a dog who belongs to anyone who speaks Mandarin or Malay.' He called loudly to the dog, '*Lie di, lie di!*' If it was going to come it wasn't going to do it in Cantonese either. Feiffer said, 'Well, how many languages are there left?'

Isandula Street, General Gordon Street, Generalissimo Chen Street.

It was nothing. It was all he had.

Feiffer, getting up and going to the door, said to the dog in Shanghainese, 'Come! Come here! Hey, boy! Come!'

The dog didn't. Feiffer said, 'O.K.?' He looked at O'Yee's face.

O'Yee said in a whisper, 'Wow.' When you knew how, there there was nothing to it. O'Yee said, still whispering, 'Wow, thanks.'

Isandula Street, General Gordon Street, Sepoy Street, Generalissimo Chen Street . . . Feiffer, pausing for a moment at the door, said with a grin, 'O.K.' He looked down at the dog and then to O'Yee. O'Yee was beaming with gratitude. Feiffer asked quietly, 'When is the family due back?'

O'Yee, shrugging and bending down to pat the dog on the head, said softly, 'Soon. I hope.' The dog was still asleep. O'Yee went on patting it.

'Soon.' O'Yee shrugged, 'I don't know. Six weeks.' O'Yee said, 'Maybe they'll get sick of America and come home early.' He leant down to pat the dog. O'Yee, looking up, said briskly, 'Don't worry about setting up the file. I'll do that.' O'Yee, predicating it on something he was far from sure of himself, said quietly, 'Thanks very much.' He said softly, more to the dog than anyone else, thinking of his family in America, 'Thanks. Thanks very much.'

German. Maybe it was a German dog.

O'Yee, squaring his shoulders as Feiffer went out of the Detectives' Room and closed the door behind him, barked down at the dog in happy expectation, 'Hund! Hund . . . *KOMMEN-SIE HIER!*'

It was The Voice Of Doom.

In the monastery garden, the monastery gardener, all his sins and omissions and paucity of Self found out from the heavens, yelled, 'Aiiya!' He was out in the sand garden, as Zen gardeners were wont to be, gardening sand. The monk, cowering and hiding his face in his hands, shrieked, 'Aiiya!' He looked up.

It wasn't The Voice Of Doom, it was The Human Fly. The Human Fly, hanging by the barest of toe and fingerholds from an eave in the crawlspace where the shot had come from, yelled down in Cantonese, 'This is Detective Inspector Auden from Yellowthread Street. Did you or did you not hear the gunshot?'

'Yes! Yes!' The monk, a tiny, wizened old man in a saffron robe, yelled without taking his hands away from his eyes, 'I heard the unity of the world disturbed, but I confess that my mind was not free and I did not let it wash over me and become part of –'

He wasn't The Human Fly, he was an eavesdropper. Any moment he was going to drop from the eave. Auden, feeling Spencer's grip on his feet starting to go, yelled down, 'What the hell are you raving about? Did you or did you not see someone up here in the crawlspace after the shot went off?' He must have. There were broken tiles all around the sand garden and at the monk's feet. Auden yelled down, 'A man in a grey suit with a full head of hair about –' Auden said in sudden rising hysteria as he felt Spencer's hands start to slip, 'Don't drop me! There isn't anything to hang onto!' He was covered in dust and burned gunpowder. Above his left shoulder the wooden gargoyles on the roof where the tiles had been shot away were

50

making creaking noises. Auden, squirming, yelled to the gardener, 'If I fall for God's sake try to catch me!'

Zen Buddhist monks didn't believe in God. The gardener, taking his hands away from his eyes for a moment and looking up, put his hands back over his eyes and refused to look up.

Auden shouted, 'He was here a moment ago. He had to crawl right by the eave to –' He was slipping. Auden, a moment before he thought he was going to go himself, yelled in desperation, 'Which way did he go?'

'That way!' The monk, pulling one hand away from his face to make an indicating finger, pointed in the general direction of Australia. The monk, starting to shake, called up to anyone who might listen, 'Our Master is still in China. We are all just novices here. We are untutored. Our learning is not perfected. We do our best, but without the guiding hand of the Master –'

Auden shrieked, *'Don't drop me!'* He heard Spencer from somewhere behind him with a firm foothold – in perfect safety – say, 'You're being too rough with him, Phil, he isn't on the same astral plane as us . . .' and Auden, gritting his teeth, called down, 'Bang. Big hole in roof. Tiles in garden. Unity of world disturbed. Person who disturbed world's unity –' He saw the gardener look up at him and quiver. Same astral plane. He wasn't even on the same bloody airline. Auden yelled down, 'Some bastard just blew a hole in your fucking roof and almost killed you! Did you or did you not see him?' He waited for more drivel about Self, sand and salvation. Auden, working himself up to his best snarl, yelled at the top of his voice – He felt Spencer's hand slip. Auden, not having to work himself up to anything, said with blind terror in his voice, 'I'm going! I'm going to fall!'

'*Yes!*' In the sand garden the sand gardener, cringing, yelled, 'Yes!' To Hell with Self. He looked up. What was in danger was self. The gardener, starting to hop, trying to find some small spot not where Auden might fall, but where his enormous bulk might *not*, shrieked, 'Yes! I saw! I heard the shot and I saw the tiles and I saw!' It looked like the man was hanging on by a thread. The gardener, all in favour of the extinction of the mind but having doubts about the desirability of the same effect on the body, shouted up in simple, naked, un-Zen, pure terror, 'Yes, I saw the gun! I heard the giggle! I saw it! I saw everything!' He managed to take one hand away from his eyes and point to the far corner of the roof where the trapdoor to the loft was. The gardener, cowering, yelled, 'That way! I heard a trapdoor! Go that way!'

The gardener, hopping back and forth on his sand, destroying in an instant all the fixed patterns of life, expectation and struggle worked intricately into it, yelled up helpfully, 'That way! That was the way the woman with the gun went! That way! I saw her!' He heard The Voice Of Doom shout, '*What?*' He heard the two hundred pound soon to destroy the world meteor yell, '*Don't drop me!*' He heard the rafter holding both The Voice Of Doom and the two hundred pound meteor start to break. He heard —

He heard Auden roar, 'What *woman?*'

The sand gardener, picking up the hem of his saffron robes with both hands in order to free his feet to flee . . .

. . . fled.

8.50 a.m. In Sepoy Street, the newspaper seller, glancing at the face of an illuminated clock advertising Seiko watches on a building at the corner of Khartoum Street, looked at The Ear Wax Man a hundred yards down the road towards the Empress Of India end of the sidewalk. The Ear Wax Man had a customer. Carefully, yet with fast, practised strokes he was bending over the man seated on a stool scraping at the built up wax with one of his little instruments. The newspaper seller had all her morning papers under her arm. Giving the load a little jerk to settle it higher, she stepped back off the sidewalk into a doorway and drew a breath.

The doorway, like all the structures in Sepoy Street — the buildings, the shopfronts and the sidewalk itself — was old and in a state of bad repair. Inside the doorway there was a flight of stairs leading to little one roomed offices and rooms. The stairs were old and in need of paint or stain and they, like the walls around them, smelled of damp and decay.

Above his customer the tall, ragged Ear Wax Man was bending down. In the strong light of the morning the newspaper seller saw the back of the man's neck bend and twist as he manoeuvred carefully to extract every gramme of wax from his customer's ear.

The newspaper seller, unlike the tall, thin Ear Wax Man, was strong and healthy. The load of newspapers in her arm weighed nothing and she did not put them down.

The Ear Wax Man's collar was ragged and grey as if, like all men who lived alone, he had never learned how to give clothes anything more than a quick, superficial rinse. His hair was thinning and dry. The newspaper seller touched her own hair. For a woman in her fifties it was still thick and well looked after. Her teeth were all her own. With the standing and walking her job entailed her feet were no good, but – with a woman's touch – she had embroidered little lotus flowers on her black slippers. She was in regular employment: the newspaper business was reliable, steady and a good provider of small but consistent profit.

And, as a Confucian – as a woman – she knew her place.

She was not pretty. There were pretty women and strong women. A man The Ear Wax Man's age, if he had wanted to, by now could have learned everything there was to know about pretty women and if he sought a woman, would seek a strong woman.

If he sought a woman at all.

The newspaper seller was anxious for a cigarette. The Ear Wax Man did not smoke and she had given it up so as not to offend him.

He never looked down the street at her. The newspaper seller, in her usual quiet spot for a nine o'clock cigarette, wondered if she might just quietly step back into the doorway to the bottom of the stairs and smoke, say, half a cigarette . . .

She was a good Confucian woman.

The Ear Wax Man did not smoke.

The newspaper seller, hefting her newspapers, ran her tongue across her lips and tried to think of something else.

The trouble with men who had reached a certain age without marrying was that they no longer liked women, or if they did, they no longer knew how to tell that a woman liked them and, cloaking their nervousness in excessive politeness, they told themselves that they preferred to live alone anyway.

The Ear Wax Man was a good worker. He was a good man. Every day he was at his spot on the street with his little stool and his polished instruments and, even if business was bad, he stayed until his appointed finishing time of six o'clock. He was consistent: a reliable man who did not drink and, judging by his clothes, was careful with himself and saved his money.

Only pretty women thought all the time of love.

The newspaper seller, fifty-eight years old and thick at the waist and with poor feet, thought of companionship and someone on the street through the day to smile at. She felt a longing, but it was not the longing of a pretty woman, it was the need of a good Confucian woman to have someone to look after.

The Ear Wax Man, finishing with his customer, unfailingly polite and deferential to the people who filled his rice bowl, straightened up and, exchanging a few words with a pleasant smile, took his payment and put it carefully into his pocket.

Behind her, in the doorway, the newspaper seller could smell the odour of damp.

It was the bitter-sweet smell of age and decay, the smell of loneliness.

She was too old and too plain to think of love.

Gazing at The Ear Wax Man's collar as he went to lean briefly on a grey electricity cable access box on the sidewalk to await his next customer, the newspaper seller felt the sharp stab of tears at the corners of her eyes.

It was not love: she was too old and too plain for that.

It was loneliness.

She was no flighty pretty girl with her head full of stupid thoughts.

She touched at her eyes with the fingers of her strong, nicotine-stained hand.

She thought about The Ear Wax Man all the time.

I am his Highness' dog at Kew;
  Pray, tell me sir, whose dog are you?
Maybe it was a Japanese dog.

In the Detectives' Room, O'Yee, holding the Station copy of the official, totally-unused 1937 edition of *Handy Phrases For English-Speaking Visitors To Japanese-Occupied China*, said with hope in his heart, '*Neko wa sinde imasu!*'

It meant, *The cat is dead.*

It was all he could find that might be of interest to a dog.

The dog made no sound at all.

It was merely waiting.

'*Neko wa sinde imasu!*' O'Yee said encouragingly, 'Aye? Does that mean anything to you at all? *Neko-wa-sinde-imasu!*' O'Yee said desperately, 'Aye? Aye? Anything? *Anything at all?*'

In Wyang Street, the man of limited time paid off his taxi and stood on the sidewalk for a long time watching the traffic. It fascinated him. Unendingly, each of the little metal boxes: the cars and vans and trucks and buses, taxis and trams went past a central point towards their destinations and, seemingly from the unceasing flow, once they were there, turned around and came back again.

He had only recently started to watch them. For years, all the vehicles, all the boxes, had gone by and he had never really seen them.

In each, there were people. There were conversations, gestures, looks, lives going past him, all self-contained and walled in as surely as if they had all been in cages.

He had never noticed it before. All his life he had lived in cities and he had never noticed the traffic.

He had never thought about it.

All his life he had lived in cities, surrounded by it, and not

55

once had he ever – not once – had he ever stopped to think deeply about it.

Now, it amazed – it fascinated him. He could not stop watching.

In Wyang Street, the man of limited time, a faint yellow stain on his fingers that had come from the kieselguhr clay he had used to make the dynamite, said softly to himself, 'Never, I never once thought about it . . .'

8.58 a.m. He had a few minutes to spare before he had to go.

The man of limited time said softly to himself, 'Never once . . .'

It was like love: a discovery.

Walking back and forth along the street, shaking his head in gentle disbelief, the man of limited time, with the eye of a convert, watched the traffic.

8.59 a.m. The Ear Wax Man was still leaning on the electricity access box waiting for customers, all his polished and well-kept little tools and scrapers laid out invitingly on the stool near his foot.

He was a good, hard working man who needed a woman to look after him.

Shutting her eyes for a moment to give herself courage and to fight the need for a cigarette, the newspaper seller, walking carefully in her embroidered black slippers so he would not know her feet were bad, went towards him, smiling.

9.00 a.m. exactly.

In Wyang Street, the man of limited time, watching, waiting, glanced at his watch.

5

9 a.m. exactly. In Sepoy Street, the newspaper seller touched at her bundle of newspapers with her free hand and tried to find somewhere to look. Watching her approach, The Ear Wax Man's eyes were full on her. She knew she waddled. She was 58 years old with a thick waist and bad feet. There was nowhere else to look except straight ahead to The Ear Wax Man. Leaning a little on the electricity access box on the sidewalk, he was watching her come with no expression on his face.

Was there no expression on his face? A truck rumbled by in the street, its engine roaring as the driver changed gears to pass a car manoeuvring to the inside lane and The Ear Wax Man, for a moment, glanced at it.

There were cars and trucks and taxis everywhere, their engines and motors roaring and revving in the narrow thoroughfare as they went towards Khartoum Street and Moore's Pocket to where they could reach the flyover and accelerate away to their places of business. In the street, the newspaper seller grimaced. When she had thought about walking to The Ear Wax Man over and over in her mind she had always imagined soft, intimate voices. The noise of the street made that impossible. Through her thin slippers she felt the shaking with all the motors and the weight of the vehicles. She was no longer a young girl. She had never been pretty.

He was watching her. His attention was full on her. He was

looking her up and down. She waddled. She knew she waddled like a duck. A short, dumpy, ugly, wrinkled old woman in a black peasant's pyjama suit hobbling on ridiculously delicately embroidered slippers to pretend that she was something other than she was, the newspaper seller closed her eyes for an instant and wished herself to be anywhere else.

If someone stopped her to buy a newspaper she would have been saved. There was no one. The street was briefly empty between the quarter to nine crowd and the quarter past and there was no one else on the sidewalk except her and The Ear Wax Man watching her.

She was alone. She had no children or grandchildren, no husband or friend or anyone to comfort her. With each step she felt herself become more and more ungainly, more and more ridiculous.

She was afraid he might laugh.

In Sepoy Street, the newspaper seller, travelling the longest fifty yards of her life, her heart and hopes in her mouth, kept walking.

In his third floor office in the Department Of Urban Development on Wyang Street, Doctor Albert Nonte glanced at his book-lined walls and, addressing them and not Feiffer, said with a trace of boredom in his voice, '*Topo*: from the Greek meaning "place", -*nomist*: one who gives names to something, hence: a namer of streets.' He was one of those now not so young Americans from the Berkeley/Viet Nam protest days, a smooth faced, but once bearded relic of the New Frontier days who, after the death of hope and idealism, had ended up far from the Front. Nonte, glancing at his framed doctorates in Chinese language and studies from both U.C.L.A and Leyden between two bookcases of reference books, said with a slight raising of his eyebrows, 'I fail to see, Mr Feiffer, what it is exactly I'm supposed to do for you.' Behind him, beneath the doctorates, there was what looked like a nineteenth century etching broken from a book on engineering. It showed the construction of Roman Roads. Nonte, shaking his head and glancing at the etching, said, shrugging, 'All I can tell you about Isandula Street and General Gordon Street – neither of which, obviously, I had anything to do with naming – is that they were built in the nineteenth century at the approximate times their names suggest, i.e. 1879 and 1885 respectively, and since then they've been progressively modernized until they're in the state you see them now.' He paused, about to sit down in his desk chair, 'What else is it you think I can tell you?'

Outside, through the window, Feiffer could see the city laid out in front of him: Hong Bay stretching down to Beach Road and Hop Pei Bay where the typhoon shelter was and, to the east, Empress Of India Street and the old Chinese cemetery that overlooked Aberdeen Road and the bay. It seemed, from that height, that there were only main landmarks in the city. There weren't. Between them, between the buildings, criss-crossing them, there was a maze of insignificant streets like Isandula and General Gordon Street. 'I simply thought you might be able to tell me something I don't know.'

'About the streets?' Nonte, still shrugging, said, 'What?' Cops, even at the remove of almost twenty years from the Berkeley days, made him nervous, 'Streets are streets. The first main system of roads and streets was built in Persia about 500 B.C., when all the provinces were connected to the capital Susa, by gangs of men working almost non stop for twenty years, the Romans built the greatest roads in Europe by about 400 B.C. and then, until the middle of the nineteenth century when the macadam process was invented for the Industrial Revolution there were no roads or streets to speak of anywhere in the world.' He was gaining confidence. He was older, more confident himself. Cops these days didn't lean on him. In a way, with his education, he could lean on them. Nonte, glancing at his watch, asked impatiently, 'What am I supposed to tell you? Why someone wanted to kill a cop?' There was a limit. He was bright enough to know that. The cops still carried the power. 'I'm sorry that your traffic policeman or whatever he was got killed, but I don't see how it's in my province –'

'They didn't want to kill a cop. They wanted to kill a street. I came to you because I think what they're after is in your province.' Feiffer, looking away from the window, said firmly, 'They're after the streets.' That had to be it. He looked at the far wall. It was covered in maps and diagrams and what looked like the family trees of thoroughfares. Feiffer said, 'Isandula Street, General Gordon Street: they both symbolize defeats and —'

'And the bombers, being great symbolists, are now going to move on to — what? Dunkirk Street and — and American Revolution Street?' Nonte, shaking his head, said, 'No. General Gordon Street, for a start, refers to Gordon's time in China, not his death in Khartoum — that would be Khartoum Street — and, as a matter of fact, Khartoum Street doesn't refer to the defeat at Khartoum at all. It refers to a contingent of Chinese Gordon took with him to the Sudan, most of whom, I might tell you, had more sense than to stay with him until he was killed by the Mahdi's fanatics, but instead, signed on with a railway company in South Africa.' He nodded at a map, 'Hence, also, Railway Street in North Point.' Nonte, tapping the map, said, 'No, if you're running away with the idea that it's some sort of action replay of, say, the Taiwanese Nationalists blowing up Mao Tse Tung Street on their national day and the Maoists blowing up Taipei Street on theirs — which happens on a regular basis — then you can forget it. No one — with the possible exception of me — would even have enough information about the meanings of half the street names to start getting symbolic about them, let alone start killing people in them.' It seemed to irritate him. 'For Christ's sake, in Chinese they're not even called Isandula and General Gordon Street.' He didn't even have to glance at his maps, 'They're The Street Of Sea Breezes and Flower Sellers' Street.' Nonte, his confidence growing by the moment, said, 'Your street: where your police station is — Yellowthread Street: originally that was where a row of fishermen's huts were before the Opium Wars that got Hong Kong for the British: that was called in the first maps End Of Life Street — what do we translate that as on a symbolic basis — Armageddon Row?' Nonte said, 'No, you're reaching.' He shrugged again, hard. 'And from what you say if someone's trying to destroy a few streets then they're not doing much of a job —'

'I didn't say they were trying to *destroy* the streets. What I said was that they were trying to kill them.'

'How? By blowing up waterpipes and chopping down parking meters? So why don't you look for goddamned Water Street or Parking Meter Street?' Nonte said, 'You're reaching. I know how you cops work, but if you think I'm going to tell you that, yes, it's some sort of dark deep secret symbolic assault on the thoroughfares of life you can forget it.' The man irritated him. 'You look for a high value load or something that's going to use one of those streets and that's where you'll find your crime.' Nonte, getting steadily more and more impatient, said, 'If you want my opinion, it's probably some sort of plan to stop an armoured car and knock it off in the middle of the street while —'

'There are no armoured cars in that area.' Feiffer, glancing out of the window for an instant to watch an aircraft passing over towards Kai Tak airport, shook his head. 'Or banks or big payroll deliveries or — in fact there's nothing in that area. All there are are streets.'

'People don't attack streets per se.'

'*Per se*, someone already has. Twice!' He was desperate. It was all he had. Feiffer, staring hard at the man, demanded angrily, 'Under the streets — you research these places — is there anything *under* either of these streets?'

'By all accounts, in Isandula Street, there used to be a water pipe but there ain't anymore.'

'Will you look it up?'

'Look what up? What are you looking for — secret tunnels? I don't even have to look it up —' Nonte, touching at his face, said, 'Yes, there are secret tunnels — they're called telephone conduits and water pipes and electricity pipes and sewer pipes and — what the hell do you want of a street? A street is a street.'

'I want to know what the hell they want.'

'Maybe all they want is to stop the traffic.'

'The traffic in General Gordon Street, with the parking meters gone, is flowing even faster than before.'

'How the hell do I know? Maybe they — whoever "they" are — just like killing people and a street just happens to be the most convenient place to —'

'On both occasions, no one was supposed to get hurt. On both occasions, what they were after —'

Nonte said, 'Was what? What in hell do you think a street *is*?'

'I don't know. What I wanted from you was —'

'Was what? My opinion on what a street is — or theirs?' Nonte said, 'I don't know. I don't know. A street is — a street.' He glanced at his degrees and, for a moment, felt a little uncomfortable. 'I don't know.'

Nonte said suddenly, 'Why are you doing this to me? I'm hiding, can't you see that? I'm a goddamned dodo from another age with three or four useless degrees in Chinese that I thought in the great days were going to make me the American Ambassador in Peking.' Nonte, rubbing hard at his face where once there had been a full beard and a life full of great plans and aspirations before the world went to hell and Viet Nam, said desperately, 'Don't ask me these sort of questions. I don't know the answers. I'm a toponomist — from the Greek *Topo*: a place and *-nomist* — I'm a namer of goddamned roads and streets, that's where I've ended up.' It all came back to him. He put his hands, for a moment, to his face.

Doctor Albert Nonte, Ph.D., on the edge of shrieking at the waste of all his life and youth and expectations, said with real fear in his eyes, 'You lousy, goddamned, fucking cop, do your own job and leave me alone!' It had all been for nothing. He was a namer of roads.

He hated the world. He hated what it had done to him.

It was 9.03.

In the third floor office overlooking the city, staring hard at the spines of the books on the shelves lining the room, searching seemingly for something that was no longer there to be found, he fell abruptly silent.

*

9.03 a.m. In Sepoy Street, as she walked, the newspaper seller, for the first time in a very long while, wished above all else that she had been born pretty.

Her feet were bad and it seemed such a very long, hard distance to walk.

The Ear Wax Man was waiting. She saw his face.

She wished someone would stop her to buy a newspaper, but there was no one.

It was such a long, hard distance to walk.

Thirty yards on Sepoy Street, Hong Bay.

It was all that separated them.

It was a man in a grey business suit. It was a woman in a silk dress.

It was a bird.

It was a plane.

It was Auden up on the roof hanging on for grim death like a squid. On the peak of the roof, crucified on hand and leg holds spread out farther than the human body was ever meant to be spread, Auden, twisting his head in order not to have it ripped off his shoulders by a vicious three inch nail the builders had forgotten to nail in when they moved the monastery from China, yelled with terror in his voice, 'Bill, *there's nothing up here.*' He twisted, this time not his head to avoid a nail, but his entire body to avoid a mound of dried pigeon dung and, talking between clenched teeth, shouted, 'It's just a roof.'

Spencer was safe in the window of the loft. It was all right for him. Auden, making funny hissing noises as the zephyrs up on the roof changed and he realised the dry dung wasn't so dry, yelled down, 'It's a tiled, sloping roof with a few carved ornaments on the supports with a line of black gargoyles or evil spirit chasers stuck on.' The evil spirit chasers weren't doing much of a job. 'I can feel the bloody dust and pollution of months up here. No one's been on this roof since it was erected.' A pigeon, released from a cage in the garden as an act of good merit by a devout Buddhist, fluttered by on its way to

63

the astral good merit plane and took a shit directly above his head. Auden, almost wrenching his neck muscles loose from their sinews to avoid it, yelled, 'What we should be doing is searching the bloody monastery.'

'We have searched the monastery. The monks have searched the monastery.' All there was in the monastery were monks. Spencer, looking concerned as Auden began sliding like the Titanic towards the edge of the roof, yelled, 'Whoever is doing the shooting is shooting at the roof! The answer lies on the roof.'

It also, supposedly, lay in the soil. Any moment Auden would be able to check out both possibilities. Auden, still sliding, yelled, 'There's nothing up here. All there are up here are a few tiles and –' A positive posse of pigeons soared past him, their digestive systems all in good working order. 'All there is up here is a bloody trainload of fucking pigeons shitting on me.' He stopped sliding down the smooth tiles for the simple reason that pigeon dung was not smooth and, making little scraping noises as the tiles became smooth again courtesy of his shirt and trousers, Auden yelled, 'It's probably just someone trying to shoot the pigeons for their bloody dinner.' He managed to look down and see the monks all out in the monastery gardens looking up at him like a box of ping pong balls. Auden, finding a hole with his free hand and hanging on to it for his life, yelled, 'Look at them. They all look bloody half starved. That's what it is, they're –'

'Buddhists don't kill things and they don't eat meat.'

'Then it's a bloody –' The only act of merit anyone was doing in the garden releasing pigeons from their cages was an act of good merit for the Acts Of Merit Man selling the pigeons. They were homing pigeons. Having taken a mass defecation on the roof on their way from the cages to freedom they were taking another on their way back from freedom to the cages again. Auden, squirming, yelled, 'What we should be doing is going through the bloody monastery guns in hand kicking bloody doors down.'

'We've already done that.'

'Then we should do it again.' Auden, ducking as something grey, white and vile landed on the roof an inch from his fingers, yelled, 'There's nothing up here. Whoever was doing the shooting is long gone and all I'm doing up here is—' He stopped. The ammonia in the bird crap had got to him. Auden, hanging in mid-air, said curiously, 'Bill, I can smell *fish*.' He looked for seagulls. There weren't any. Auden, twisting his head first one way and then the other on the roof, looking nonplussed, said with a confused look on his face, 'I can smell fish and the smell's getting closer.' Under his face, the tiles were all solid and unbroken. He rubbed at them with his forehead. 'I can smell fish and it's getting –' He looked down to the upturned faces of the monks in the courtyard. 'I can smell the smell of fish and it's getting closer and closer –' Auden said, 'Bill, something's getting close to me up here and it smells of –' He said suddenly, 'And gunpowder and incense and – I can smell the smell of –' He saw, just for an instant, the muzzle of the Chinese hand cannon poke its snout through a broken tile in the roof not twenty feet away as he called down in terror, 'Bill! Bill! It's –' He could see what the gun was going to shoot at. He saw it. Auden, grabbing hold of anything and every-thing – hard, soft and dungy – that might just for that fraction support him as the entire roof shook and trembled with the gunshot and the smoke enveloped him, yelled, 'I see it. It's up there. I can see what they're shooting at.'

Auden, ruined, injured, scraped, lacerated and still shaking, yelled down, 'I saw it. I saw the target. It was a round, golden disc. It was –'

It was the sun.

Auden said softly, 'Oh, shit . . .' and, obligingly aiming with unerring precision at his upturned face, through the ris-ing acrid white smoke, one of the wheeling, panic-stricken pigeons . . . did.

Why not simply put an ad in the newspaper informing the reading public that their lost dog was found and could be picked up to their happiness and joy in the Detectives'

Room of the good old reliable dog-finding and owner happiness-bringing Yellowthread Street Police Station, Hong Bay?

How much could it cost?

O'Yee opened the phone book classifieds at Newspapers.

He glanced at the dog.

He glanced at the no less than ninety-seven newspapers in no less than nineteen different languages.

He glanced at the dog.

Maybe it was an Italian dog.

O'Yee, opening his desk dictionary at the back, said indefatigably in Latin, '*In rebus asperis et tennui spe fortissima quaeque consilia tutissima sunt.*'

He asked the dog hopefully, 'Well? *Anything?*'

Nothing.

O'Yee said quietly, 'Hmm.' He furrowed his brow to think.

To be fat in the province her family came from in China was not a humiliation. People greeted each other with compliments on how fat they were growing.

It was a good thing, a symbol of a calm mind and prosperity in business. In Shensi province when she had been a girl the compliment 'You are fatter' had meant –

It was the West with all its ideas of what women should look like that had changed everything.

The newspaper seller, conscious of her thickening, ugly waist, said softly to herself in Shensi dialect, 'You are fatter.'

It was a compliment.

She saw The Ear Wax Man looking at her.

All around her was the sound of the traffic.

'You are fatter.'

It was a compliment.

It was a compliment!

At 9.05 a.m. on Sepoy Street, approaching The Ear Wax Man, all she wanted to do was run away.

*

In Wyang Street, at his car, Feiffer paused. In Chinese, Wyang Street, at least was still called Wyang Street.

Symbols.

A wyang was a Chinese opera, the symbols in that: the stylized make-up and costumes — unchanged for a thousand years.

Symbols.

Isandula Street. General Gordon Street.

What it all meant was nothing.

It was a game, a challenge: it meant nothing.

He wondered.

Standing by his car with the traffic moving unstoppably, cacophonously all around him, going nowhere, doing nothing, meaning *zero*, Feiffer wondered desperately what in God's name he could possibly do next.

He was smiling at her. In Sepoy Street, as she reached him, she saw The Ear Wax Man smile. He was smiling, wonderfully. By the electricity cable box he had straightened up and he was looking at her full on and seeing only her face and he was smiling at her. There were customers coming. She saw one of them pluck at his sleeve and she saw him smiling at her and he looked for only a fraction of a moment to his customer — to that which was the most important thing in his life — and she saw him shake his head to the man and look back to her smiling.

The newspaper seller, stopping, feeling her hands shake, smiling back, said in Shensi dialect, 'I — I hope you are well —' and he was still smiling at her and coming towards her.

He was a hard working, good, clean man. She was 58 years old with bad feet and a thick ugly waist. *'You are fatter.'* It was a compliment. He was speaking Shensi: he had learned it for her and he was walking towards her smiling with a wonderful look on his face.

'You are fatter.' He had learned it for her. Above the sound of the traffic, she heard it. He was looking a little concerned,

67

wondering if he had said it the right way. The newspaper seller said, nodding, in Cantonese, 'Yes, yes, that's right.'

'You are fatter.' He was beaming, happy. He had got it right. He was smiling at her. Over and over, like a child pleasing someone, the Ear Wax Man was saying in Shensi, 'You are fatter.' The Ear Wax Man said in Cantonese, 'You are beautiful.'

She had walked all the way to him the way a Confucian woman would. The newspaper seller, holding her income and her worth and her dowry under her arm, said in Cantonese, 'I work hard.' She looked at The Ear Wax Man and his wonderful, lined face. 'As do you.' The newspaper seller, looking down for a moment to her embroidered slippers, said quietly, 'I – these slippers. They are my work.'

'Yes.' There were customers, two of them. They paused for a moment. The Ear Wax Man, with a shake of his head, sent them away. The Ear Wax Man, reaching into the pocket of his ragged jacket, took out a single cigarette. The Ear Wax Man said softly, still smiling, 'I know you smoke cigarettes.' He was smiling, wonderfully. The Ear Wax Man said –

It was the moment. On his wrist the second hand reached its zenith on his watch face and at exactly 9.12 a.m. it was the moment.

In Wyang Street the man of limited time drew a breath.

It was the moment.

9.09 a.m.

Precisely.

Exactly . . .

The Ear Wax Man said –

By him, somewhere in the grey metal electricity access box by his elbow, The Ear Wax Man heard a click.

It was only a millisecond: the space between words.

In Sepoy Street, The Ear Wax Man, smiling, said with hope, 'I have waited for such a long –'

Exactly.

In Wyang Street, even before he heard it and saw the flash, the man of limited time felt the tremor. It was more than a tremor, it was a surge, a boost, a roar of power. It was wonderful, a release, a burst of awesome, pent-up joy and liberation.

He heard it.

He heard the explosion.

He saw the smoke and then, reflected against all the windows and against all the buildings, he felt the detonation as, exactly on time, to the moment, to the second, to the fraction – exactly on time – Sepoy Street, Hong Bay, in the British Crown Colony of Hong Kong, totally and utterly, completely, ceased to exist.

6

In Sepoy Street all the burglar alarms were ringing and ringing. With their electrical supply blasted out under the roadway they were on automatic battery power and they were going to go on ringing and ringing until someone got to them one by one and cut them off.

The cars blown apart by the explosions of their own petrol tanks were still on fire, turning white as the Fire Brigade doused them in foam and, with the force of the jets, set them rocking and moving and directed the black, oily poisonous smoke from their smouldering electrical conduits and seats billowing and rising.

The ambulancemen had got all the bodies free and laid them out on the sidewalk in a row. They were not bodies, they were burned black, charred logs. In Sepoy Street, the red hot shrapnel blasted out from the electrical access box had ripped through the bodies and the cars and incinerated them. They were not bodies laid out on the sidewalk: they were black logs. There were eleven of them. The logs, here and there, had branches. They were arms locked in pugilistic position above the blackened faces, as in their last moments, the fire had come down the street and overwhelmed them.

In Sepoy Street, the Commander said softly, 'God Almighty . . .' He looked at Feiffer standing next to him and saw the face of an old man. There were no words. Down the entire length of the street there were people working, but with the alarms they seemed to work in silence and there were no words. The Commander, touching at his face and looking down at the ground, said softly to himself, 'God Almighty . . .'

Half in and half out of the crater where the electrical access box had been, Technical Inspector Matthews, on his hands and knees, yelled above the noise, 'Dynamite. Some sort of dynamite formulation – about, I estimate – thirty pounds of it fitted to a timing device, probably based on nothing more elaborate than an alarm clock with a six volt battery and an electrical detonator.' He had to shout above the sound of the alarms and the compressors the Fire Brigade were using, 'I can smell nitro residue down here: it was some sort of home made dynamite using low-grade nitroglycerine made in someone's freezer soaked into kieselguhr clay to give it temporary stability and handling qualities and then placed here sometime in the middle of the night.' All you needed to open an electricity access hatch or any roadway manhole not designed to be tamper-proof was a simple T key that could be made in five minutes with a length of three eights inch steel rod and a flat file. 'The incendiary effect came from pieces of red hot metal striking passing vehicles and ripping open their petrol tanks.' He got his head completely down into the hole and then, popping up again with a look of triumph on his face, yelled, 'Yeah, I can see burns on some of the remaining foundation stones where the acid from the nitro leaked out.' He could smell the smell of death in the street. Matthews, drawing a long flashlight from the pocket of his coveralls like a sword, yelled, 'I'll get down into the hole with a light and see what I can find.'

The bodies, eleven of them, laid out on the sidewalk didn't look like bodies. Except for the colour and the smell they could have been statues. The Commander, lighting a cigarette, said softly, 'How many injured?' He looked at Feiffer's face.

'Thirty-one.' In the centre of the street near where the Fire Brigade tenders were, there were the black death-wagons from the Mortuary. They were waiting for the firemen to finish. Feiffer, glancing away, said above the sound of the alarms, 'At least four of them won't make it to the hospital.' When he had got there, the injured were still lying in the street. They had been screaming. The sound was still in his ears. After the first ten the morphine had run out and the ambulancemen had had to wait for more supplies to be brought up in a car. Feiffer, blinking in the black smoke, said without looking at the Commander, 'There's nothing —' In the centre of the road he saw Arthur Collins of the Main Roads Department wandering, lost, between the burned out cars and the debris. He seemed to be crying. Feiffer said with an effort at concentration, 'There's nothing I can do. There's nothing to ask anyone — nothing.' He looked hard at the Commander and saw that the man was ashen-faced and trembling. 'It just went off and killed everyone.' He looked at the crater in the sidewalk where the access box had been and saw only flashes of light as, somewhere down there, Matthews, at least, was safe from the awful smell. 'Anyone who might have seen anything is dead.' He looked at the run-down shops and buildings on either side of the street. 'At night, no one comes here. It's — it's just a lane. No one ever comes here —'

The Commander was not smoking the cigarette in his hand. He was looking at it because there was nowhere else he wanted to look. He was not going to smoke it. It was merely something to hold in his hand and look at. Feiffer said with an effort at control, 'Two of them — two of them who were standing closest to it appear to be holding hands.' He felt something in his face tighten. He was having difficulty framing the words. 'They appear to have been —' Feiffer said suddenly, 'I don't even know what sex they were. I found an embroidered woman's slipper but I don't even know which of them it belongs to.' He was shaking, losing control, 'It took both their heads off, Neal — both of them. It went through their bodies like a goddamned mincer.' They were there somewhere among the black, dead logs: parts of them — what was left of them. Feiffer, trembling, said above the sound of the alarms, 'They were burned black and I don't even —'

'I know.'

72

'You don't bloody know!' When he had arrived the injured were still screaming and in one of the burning cars, there was a man trapped with his face and chest on fire. The street was gone, torn to pieces. In a moment, it had been turned into a charnel-house. Feiffer, watching Collins wandering through the rubble searching for something that might resemble some part of a street he and his Main Roads gangs might be able to put back together, said, 'Nobody bloody knows. The only people who bloody know are the people who did this.' The stench of the dead was overwhelming. It was sweet, heavy. It was everywhere. In the road, Collins, reeling like a drunk, put his hand to his head and seemed to stagger. Feiffer, shaking his head, said, 'No. No, it's too much. Whatever they're doing – whatever they're doing it for – it's too much doing this.' In the street the alarms were ringing and ringing. The sound seemed to be coming from inside his head. Feiffer, trying to look away, as, in the centre of the street, Collins put his hand to his face and wept, said, 'What the hell am I supposed to do about this? *What the hell am I supposed to do about this?*'

'I don't know.'

'Matthews says it's a bloody *game!*'

'I don't know, Harry.'

'Matthews says it's a bloody game! They cut P.C. Lo's fucking *hands* off! They almost killed two people in Isandula Street! And now this! And bloody Matthews says it's a bloody game!' The terrible, awful smell was everywhere. 'They've got bloody dynamite and thermite and bloody – and God knows what concoctions they're putting together somewhere and they're doing it for no reason at all!' The dead looked like black, twisted logs. They were not people, they were inanimate twisted objects. They had never had life. They had never meant anything. They were merely black objects. Two of the dead had been holding hands. He had found a single embroidered slipper. It had been Shensi province work. He had known that. In the street, Arthur Collins from Main Roads was weeping. It was more than the ambulancemen had time for. In the midst of the screaming and the terrible cries for help they had run out of morphine. Feiffer demanded, 'Why? Why are they doing this? What in the name of all that's holy is it *for*?' The Fire Brigade was working on the last of the burning cars. When it was out and the area declared safe he would have to go forward with the Government Medical Officer and the men from the death-wagons from the Mortuary to examine the bodies one by one. Feiffer, watching Collins in the middle of the street, wishing he too, could find tears, said in total, utter desperation, '*Why*? What is it for? Neal, for God's sake, why is this happening?'

He saw someone come through the smoke from the other end of the street and stand for a moment near Collins and then look over to where the bodies were. It was Henry Yu from the Hong Bay Alarm Company. For a moment, he seemed to be about to touch Collins on the shoulder to console him.

His cigarette still untouched in his hand, the Commander, watching as the fire in the last burning car was doused and the Fire Brigade approached it with only hand extinguishers to declare it safe, said softly, 'Harry . . .'

It was Henry Yu from the alarm company. He was wearing a grey dust coat and looked down the street to where the bodies were. In the centre of the street Collins was weeping with his hand over his eyes. He seemed to be stooped over, aged. The smell was everywhere. Laid out on the sidewalk were the dead.

It was something. It was something to do.

In the street, Collins was weeping.

The death-wagons were lined up, waiting. Inside them, the stretcher bearers and porters were putting their white face masks on ready to go forward.

The fire was out in the last burning car.

They were only the dead. They had no meaning. They had never been alive. Whatever they had been or ever wanted to be was all for nothing.

It was a game. It was nothing more than a game. Technical Inspector Matthews said so. It was a game.

'Harry . . .'

He watched as the people from the death-wagons began to cross the road to where the bodies were.

There were no words.

In the centre of the road, Henry Yu from the alarm company put out his hand to touch Collins on the shoulder to say something.

There were no words.

They were the living. They had things to do.

Nodding to Feiffer as he came forward with a set, terrible expression on his face, Henry Yu from the Hong Bay Alarm Company, taking his little packet of tools from the pocket of his grey dust coat, steeling himself against what he would see on the way, went towards the far end of the street to begin turning off all the alarms.

It was crazy. There was no way on Earth that it should work, but it was. It was working. In the centre of the pedestrian overpass above the Hong Bay flyover that linked all of Hong Bay to the Central District of Hong Kong and thence to the ferries and tunnel that serviced the route to Kowloon, Chief Inspector Kyle-Foxby said softly, 'It's crazy.'

With Isandula Street closed and all the parking meters gone in General Gordon Street and now, Sepoy Street blocked off, there should have been no way that the flow of traffic should have remained constant below him.

The traffic flow was constant. Below him, on the flyover and, behind that, in all the streets of Hong Bay, the vehicles: the trucks, cars, vans, buses were moving at their top, optimum circulation and there were no hold ups at all.

It was crazy. If he had had a month of computer time he could not have arranged it better: the closed streets made no difference at all – for all the difference they made to the flow they could have been totally non-existent.

It was crazy. It was impossible to close a street in Hong Kong and not have the traffic all over the island grind to an instant, solid halt. It was impossible. All the studies proved it.

On the overpass, staring down at the moving stream below him, Kyle-Foxby said curiously into his walkie-talkie to the radar speed trap car he had permanently set up a mile down the road, 'Am I right in assessing an accelerated circulation, Constable?' He always spoke English to his Chinese constables. It bettered their chances for promotion. Kyle-Foxby, waiting for the words to be slowly translated and made sense of, said, 'Well?'

'Yes, sir.' The disembodied voice was calm, business-like and unemotional. 'Speed of traffic increased.' The Chinese accent was too strong. The word 'speed' came out as 'spleed.'

Kyle-Foxby said to correct it, ' "Speed", Constable, the word is prounounced "speed".'

He couldn't understand it. The traffic, far from being disrupted, was flowing even faster.

It irritated him.

He couldn't understand it at all.

10.18 a.m.

With his elbow on the railing of the overpass, gazing down, Chief Inspector Kyle-Foxby B.A. tapped his nose gently with his finger and stood watching the traffic, deep in thought.

This was what a friend was for – to do the brain work. It was a team. When you had a friend you had a team. You had someone who considered you. In the grounds of the monastery watching as more idiots did more acts of good merit by releasing pigeons from cages, that, as soon as your back was turned, flew back to the cages, Auden said happily, 'Now we sit down somewhere comfortable and work it out – right, Bill?' He had climbed, clambered, clung and conquered. He had been a friend. Auden watching as people came in from the street and paid good money for nothing, said, 'I know you've been thinking about it all.' He was still hopping slightly from his various injuries. Spencer was a man who had deep thoughts. Auden, glancing around for a bench, said enthusiastically, 'Where do we sit?'

Where you sat was where the man in the grey business suit or the woman in the silk dress was shooting. Spencer looked up.

Auden said, 'Oh, no.'

Spencer said slowly, 'Hmm . . .' He put his hand gently on Auden's shoulder.

Auden said, 'Oh, *no* . . .'

There was a glint in Spencer's eyes. It was the glint of brain work, of intelligence, of friendship.

Auden, still hopping, said, 'Oh – *no*.'

In the Detectives' Room, O'Yee, looking at the Polaroid pictures of the dead and inserting them carefully into the file, said softly, 'Sepoy Street – it commemorates the Sepoy Mutiny of 1857 when the Indian soldiers in the East India Company's Bengal Army mutinied against their officers and slaughtered them.' He looked across to where Feiffer sat at his own desk patting the dog. O'Yee, glancing back through the file, said quietly, 'Isandula Street, General Gordon Street, Sepoy Street – they're all defeats of one sort of another.' He looked at Feiffer's face. He seemed very tired and old. His hand, not so much patting as resting on the dog's head was stroking one way and then another, ruffling the dog's coat, caressing it. O'Yee asked, 'Would you like some coffee, Harry?'

The dog was awake, resting on its hind legs, its head in Feiffer's lap, making little groaning noises. With all the Uniformed men still out in Sepoy Street on house to house, in the Station there was only the sound of the clock. With the windows closed, there was barely any sound of traffic at all. At his desk, leaning down a little to reach it, Feiffer's hand went back and forth along the dog's coat. The dog raised its head a little and laid it down for Feiffer to work on. The dog's eyes were open, brown and liquid. Feiffer, smiling, said, 'No, thanks.' He looked at the open file on O'Yee's desk. 'They're beating me, Christopher.' It was 12.06 and he had been back from the Mortuary for over twenty minutes without saying more than six words. 'We're not even playing the same game.' He looked down at the dog and gave its ears a gentle tug, 'There were two or three people that the ambulancemen thought might make it to the hospital alive, but they didn't. While I was in the Mortuary they brought them in too.'

O'Yee said, 'What's that make it?' He glanced down at Feiffer's notes in the file. 'Fourteen?'

'Fourteen.' After they had treated the first ten of the injured in the street the ambulancemen had run out of morphine and had to send back for more. Feiffer said softly, 'And Lo – fifteen.' He had a cigarette in the ashtray on his desk. He took it up and, leaning back in the chair, inhaled it deeply. The smoke, curling away towards the closed windows, billowed about his face. Feiffer said to no one in particular, 'Fifteen.' He looked down at the dog wanting him to go on stroking it and gave it a gentle pat on the head. Feiffer said, 'Two of them – what was left of them – two of them were holding hands. They were street people.'

'Do you want some coffee, Harry?' O'Yee looked down at the Polaroid photographs. None of the dead had faces. O'Yee, brightening, said quickly, 'I've tried almost every language under the sun on the bloody dog and so far all I can get in response is a sort of Universal Woof.'

It was a dog. It had no language. On Feiffer's lap, it did what all dogs did: it beamed up at whoever was patting it.

'I've got nothing.' Feiffer, looking at the cigarette in his hand and shaking his head, not talking to O'Yee at all, not even in the room, but still back in the street, said in a whisper, 'Nothing at all. I haven't got one thing I can go on.' He looked down at the dog. His hand stroking it back and forth was so gentle as to be sending the dog to sleep where it lay. 'I couldn't do anything in the street to help those people and I can't do anything now.' He looked suddenly exhausted and drawn. Feiffer said, still in a whisper, 'And Lo – well, at least we knew who he was.'

'I'll get you some coffee, Harry.'

'Thanks.' Feiffer, looking up, said as if it was the first time the offer had been made, 'Thanks very much.'

It was a dog. It was an ordinary, simple, run-of-the-mill, even-tempered, big mongrel dog. It had life, warmth. Like all dogs, when you were low, it knew how to put its head on your lap to be stroked.

O'Yee, starting to rise, said softly, 'Harry –'

O'Yee saw Feiffer look down at the sleeping dog and smile.

O'Yee said cheerfully, 'Good dog, that.'

He was glad he had had something worthwhile to offer.

He went out into the next room to make the coffee and leave Feiffer and the dog alone together for a while.

At 12.09 p.m., the man of limited time, on duty in Sepoy Street, glanced at his watch. The dead had all been taken away and behind the barriers there were only the people from Scientific and a few uniformed Constables still working.

The man of limited time was also there on duty. He, like everyone else who had something to contribute, had been called in to do what he was best at.

The man of limited time smiled to himself.

He was an official, one of the forces of law, order and Establishment.

There was still the smell of smoke and rubber from the cars in the street, but it bothered him not at all.

Dynamite. If he put his hand to his nose he could still just make out the smell of the kieselguhr on his fingers.

It was like the dust mask he had kept from Isandula Street. It was a souvenir.

12.10 p.m.

At his official task – doing what he got paid for – the man of limited time, humming to himself, continued making his plans.

7

'I'm up on the roof and he's downstairs in the monastery because I'm a bloody ignoramus, that's why – if you really want to know.' Auden, perched on the roof with the broken tiles, the pigeon dung and the gargoyles, shouted down to the Acts Of Merit Man in the monastery courtyard, 'I'm a bloody blunt instrument, so obviously I get all the good blunt jobs while he gets to walk around sucking on his bloody meer-schaum pipe working it all out like bloody Sherlock Holmes – all right?' He was speaking Cantonese. The Acts Of Merit Man gazed up at him. Auden, in an orgy of ignoramus-facing, yelled out, 'O.K.? Is that all right? Got that, have you?'

The Acts Of Merit Man had his pigeons to keep him company. The Acts Of Merit Man, nodding, yelled back, 'Who's Sherlock Holmes?'

'Judge bloody Dee then.' The main gates to the monastery had been closed and all the monks were lined up in the grounds like yellow wine bottles waiting to be drunk. The first one to smirk was in a lot of trouble. Auden, putting his hand onto a tile to get a better purchase and then getting pigeon crap and taking it away again, yelled down to anyone who might listen, 'I'm not capable of working out why a man in a grey business suit or a woman in a silk dress is shooting tiles off a roof, I just have to sit on the bloody roof like some sort of bloody bathing beauty and look pretty.' Auden, squirming to get a broken tile away from a vital artery in his ruined ankle, yelled down, 'You're religious. You don't need to worry about other people – you can just go on happily by yourself.'

The Acts Of Merit Man was a little old Chinese wearing a blue skull cap and a blue jacket above the traditional yellow underskirt. He had a kind face. Auden, switching from Cantonese to English, said, 'I need a friend.' He felt hot tears in his eyes, 'I've reached that certain age when you get tired of yourself and what you need –' He was talking to the gargoyles on the roof. Auden, feeling sorry for himself, said in English –

In the front courtyard the little old man with the kind face said in English, 'Yes, one comes to a closed door in one's life and the man behind it, without a key, is oneself.'

Auden said, 'What?' Spencer was somewhere inside the deserted monastery with – the theory went – only the man in the grey suit and/or the woman in the silk dress to keep him company. Auden, glancing around in case he had misheard, said again, in English, 'What?'

The Acts Of Merit Man even had a queue: a pigtail. He was a Chinese of the old school. The Acts Of Merit Man, pausing only for a moment to tap reassuringly at one of the wickerwork cages his pigeons lived in, said, still in English, 'If the heart be not wounded, the eyes will not weep.' His pigeons were all homing pigeons. Any act of merit you did by releasing one of them to freedom pleased only his bank manager. Auden, scratching at his head, said, 'Right.'

He even carried a walking stick. The Acts Of Merit Man, not a day under eighty-five, called out, 'Our pleasures are shallow, our troubles deep.' He looked up encouragingly.

Auden, shrugging, said, 'Right.' He wasn't an ignoramus. He could understand proverbs with the best of them. Auden, leaning down a little over the peak and nodding, yelled back –

The Acts Of Merit Man, looking alarmed, yelled up, 'Be careful.'

Auden yelled down, 'Judge not lest ye be judged.' Auden yelled down, 'The Bible.'

Obviously the monks could not understand English. There

were no walls to gaze at so they had taken up gazing down at their feet. The Acts Of Merit Man called up, still in English, 'A *tou* of rice is not a *pao* of rice. Mandarin proverb.' He raised a gnarled finger, 'One pao is five tou, you see.' He smiled.

'Right.' He tried to think. Auden, touching his finger to his mouth, demanded, 'What is the sound of one hand clapping?' Somewhere inside the monastery his so-called friend was stalking up and down the corridors going 'Hmm, hmm.' You didn't need 'Hmm, hmm' from a real friend. What you needed from a real friend was conversation. Auden called down, 'Zen Buddhism.'

'Ah.' He was at least eighty-five years old. He had been around. The Acts Of Merit Man called up with a shrug, 'There is nothing much to Zen Buddhism.'

'I read that.' Auden, almost slipping off the roof, yelled down, 'I read that in a book about it. That's what they said.' A bit of encouragement: that was what your average ignoramus needed. Show him a bit of concern — a modicum of respect for his views — and you might discover he wasn't an ignoramus at all. The birds, all fifty or sixty of them, were each in little wickerwork cages waiting for repentant souls to come along and pay to release them to earn a little consideration in the next world. Auden, understanding, yelled down, 'It matters not at all that the birds return, it is the act of generosity that is paramount.' He understood. He nodded at the price tags on the cages, 'A man must live.' He dimly recalled something from school about indulgences and nailing bits of paper to church doors. Auden yelled down, 'Here I stand. I can do no other.'

'They shoot at nothing. They shoot only at the reflection of themselves. The true target is oneself.' The Acts Of Merit Man, pointing up at the roof, said in explanation, 'The people with the guns.'

Auden said, 'Oh. Right.'

'Zen Buddhism in the Art of Archery.'

He would have preferred to have read that one to the one he had got, but it had been out of the library at the time. Auden, feeling slighted, said, 'I didn't read it.'

'Does a bird read when he takes to the air or does he simply, merely, because it is his nature, take to the air?' (Speaking of birds, Auden could smell the smell of fish on the roof. It came and went with the breeze.) 'If a man be not enlightened within, what lamp shall he light? If his intentions are not upright, what prayers shall he repeat?' The Acts Of Merit Man, his kind face smiling, glanced at the row of monks. The Acts Of Merit Man called up in English, 'For one son who becomes a priest, nine generations get to Heaven.'

The monks were still gazing at their feet. Auden, sliding a little down the roof to drop his voice, couldn't have agreed more. Auden, his heart softening, said with a patting motion in the air that forgave all transgressions, 'I always thought Zen Buddhists went around hitting each other to gain Enlightenment.'

'True.' The Acts Of Merit Man, still nodding at Auden's sagacity, said sadly, 'They have no Master so they think they cannot find mastery.'

Right. He would have laid odds on that one too. Auden, still smelling fish, said slowly, 'He is a good fellow who can endure wrong.' It was the one proverb he knew in both Cantonese and Mandarin. Auden, still sliding down the roof, called down, 'Ch'ih te k'uei shih 'hao 'han.'

The Acts of Merit Man called up curiously, 'What can they be shooting at? If there is nothing for the inept man to aim at how can he ever learn to aim at nothing?'

The monks were a pretty sorry lot. They were not even monks. They were novices. They were still learning. In Zen Buddhism the Master went around hitting them to . . . They had no Master. They were not being hit. They gazed at walls and got nowhere. There was nothing on the roof except pigeon dung and the smell of fish. That and broken tiles and gargoyles and . . . and pigeon dung and . . . Somewhere in the monastery Spencer was going, 'Hmm, hmm . . .'

In the courtyard the Acts Of Good Merit Man called up, 'In learning, length of study goes for nothing; the most intelligent becomes master.'

'As man must eat knowledge, what then must a –'

The Acts Of Merit Man called up, smiling, 'You made that one up.'

'Then must a –'

The Acts Of Merit Man, still smiling, said, nodding, 'But that is not a disgrace. There is nothing much in proverbs.' He looked at his cages. 'There is nothing much in acts of good merit. There is nothing much in –' The Acts Of Merit Man called up a moment before Auden could ask, 'And pigeons' guts: what naturally inhabits pigeons' guts?'

'Fish.'

On the roof, standing up, shouting it to the heavens, Auden yelled, 'Fish.'

Auden, standing up, straddling the roof like a mental colossus, taking off his coat and holding it above his head like a standard, yelled in an ecstasy that sent the lined-up, hand-clasping monks fleeing back into the monastery like terrified canaries, 'Bill! Bill! Fish! Fish!' He was no ignoramus. He was a Titan. He saw Spencer come out from one of the little wooden doors looking alarmed. He saw the Acts Of Merit Man smile.

Auden, standing on the roof still waving his coat, yelled in ecstasy, 'Fish! Fish! What it is is *fish*!'

Auden, still straddling, still coat swinging, still yelling, in a paroxysm of joy, shrieked at the top of his voice, 'There isn't much to Zen Buddhism!' He saw Spencer staring up at him in total confusion.

Auden shouted down, 'Fish! Fish! Don't you see? Fish!!' He shouted down, 'I've solved it! I've solved it all!' He shouted down, 'All we have to do now is catch a pigeon and – very gently, not too viciously – bloody *murder* it!'

So simple.

Auden shouted down, 'You see? Novices without a Master! Hand cannons! Fish!'

Poor dumb ignoramus.

He saw Spencer gaze up at him, totally nonplussed.

84

Auden said with his eyes narrowed in happy, liberated anticipation, *'Hah!'*

In Sepoy Street, the man of limited time, getting on with his work, nodded to one of the cops from Scientific as he passed by and lit a cigarette.

His official work was almost done. The man of limited time nodded to himself.

It was perfect. Except for something he had seen in the street when the bodies had still been there, everything had been perfect.

Except for something he had seen in the street when the bodies had been there everything had been planned, estimated, reckoned and executed faultlessly and with precision.

Except for something he had seen in the street . . .

Perhaps it was nothing.

The man of limited time, smoking his cigarette, glanced at his watch.

1 p.m. exactly.

He had seen something in the street he had not liked and it worried him.

He had seen someone *do* something.

He looked at his watch.

There was still time.

If it was wrong he could fix it.

It was planned. It was perfect.

In Sepoy Street, smoking his cigarette, gazing at the ruins of the street, the man of limited time was sure.

If it was wrong he could fix it.

He was never wrong.

He was certain.

Isandula Street, General Gordon Street, Sepoy Street . . . They were blocks apart at the eastern end of the district leading, on their own accounts, nowhere except to the new flyover that linked Hong Bay to the Central District of Hong Kong and then, from Central via the tunnel or the ferries across the harbour to Kowloon.

Isandula Street, General Gordon Street, Sepoy Street, Peking Road, Soochow Street, Moore's Pocket, Khartoum Street: they were streets, thoroughfares, lanes – they were marks on a map.

They were nothing.

At this desk, Feiffer, gazing at the closed file on O'Yee's desk, said quietly, 'Streets . . .' There was absolutely nothing of value in any of them.

There was nothing, nothing at all. Whoever they were – five of them if The Embarrassment Man, half blind, had counted the shadows properly – all they were doing was destroying the streets themselves.

The streets led nowhere, meant nothing.

They were nothing but marks on a map.

Streets.

Streets full of black, burned away, unidentifiable logs.

1.05 p.m.

He had been avoiding it for as long as he could.

With the dog padding quietly after him, Feiffer, his face set, went across the room, to look, again, at the terrible, meaningless, Polaroid photographs of the dead.

He wondered.

In Sepoy Street, the man of limited time, smoking his cigarette, wondered.

'It's a question of evidence.' The Acts Of Merit Man had his hand on the catch of the first wickerwork pigeon cage. On that hand, Spencer's hand also rested. Spencer, trying to make someone understand, said urgently, 'Look, consider the evidence –'

The Acts Of Merit Man considered it. The Acts Of Merit Man, taking his hand from under Spencer's paw and resting it on the top of the cage to soothe the pigeon inside, said with a nod, 'Yes.' He smiled, 'So far the evidence is that your friend believes you to think him an ignoramus.' He looked up to where Auden was happily climbing to the peak of the roof and smelling gargoyles as he went. 'So far the evidence is that he thinks you hold him in little esteem because he is big, red-faced and stupid.' The Acts Of Merit Man was not a day under eighty-five. In all that time he had learned not to make snap judgements. The Acts Of Merit Man said, 'Of course, you might be right.'

'I'm not right. I don't think he's red-faced or an ignoramus. It's just that –' Auden was almost at the peak. He had his coat dragging behind him like a security blanket. Any moment now he was going to demand the mass release of the pigeons. Spencer, looking uncomfortable, said with a chopping motion of his hands, 'It's just that he was the best man for the job.'

On the roof, Auden, happily sniffing, yelled back over his shoulder, 'Zen Buddhist monastery, ha! How can it be a Zen Buddhist monastery when there is no Master? How can there be no Master if it is a Zen Buddhist monastery?' It was all only too clear. He was going to catch a few pigeons. He had gone mad. The ammonia in the pigeon dung had got to him. Auden, still clambering, still raving, yelled, 'See, Bill, once you penetrate to the fact that everything is nothing and nothing is everything, everything becomes something.' It wasn't the ammonia from the bird dung, it was the incense coming up through the roof tiles. He even spoke with a Tibetan accent. Auden, reaching the peak and straddling it, yelled down, 'There isn't much to Zen Buddhism, but what there is to Zen Buddhism at least has to be Zen Buddhism.' He called down, 'Man in a grey business suit, young woman in a silk dress – *ha*! Why not an elephant in a bloody tutu or a rhinoceros with pearls?'

In the courtyard, Spencer, wilting under the silence from the Acts Of Merit Man, said softly, defiantly, 'He went up there on the roof because he has a habit of –'

The Acts Of Merit Man smiled. He knew Spencer was going to say something bad. The Acts Of Merit Man, looking concerned, put his finger to his lips and glanced up at Auden.

87

He wasn't going to say something bad. Spencer, hopping from one foot to the other, taking his hand away from the wickerwork cage, said in desperation, 'It's just that he has a habit of hitting people.'

The Acts Of Merit Man said, 'Ah.' He looked up to where Auden was perching himself on the roof and laying out his coat like a net. The Acts Of Merit Man said sadly, 'What a burden it is to carry a man who wishes to be your friend and is not worthy of it.' He asked, 'What do you think he could mean by saying that the man in the grey business suit and the woman in silk do not exist?' He asked, 'Is that, in his stupid way, what he is saying?'

That was what, in his stupid way, he was saying. He was also about to say, 'Release the pigeons.' Spencer, making a face, said, 'No, that isn't what he's saying.'

'Then what is he saying?'

'He's saying that he thinks that —' Spencer looked up. 'He's saying that — he's saying that since the monks' Master is still in China that they're not behaving like monks at all and that they're lying to us about the man and the woman.' He looked up. Was that what he was saying? Spencer said, 'Hmm.' Spencer said, 'He's saying that —' Spencer said suddenly, 'He's saying that his so-called friend sent him up onto the roof because he's stupid when, in fact, his so-called friend —' Auden was perched. He was big and red-faced. Spencer said desperately, ashamed, 'He's saying that I —'

Auden yelled down happily, 'Ready, Bill?'

Spencer, hopping, said, *'All right.'* He saw Auden stand up and, for an instant, almost lose his balance and topple over into eternity. Spencer said, 'Phil —.' He was big and red-faced. He was — He saw Auden teeter and regain his balance. Spencer yelled out, *'I'm afraid of heights.* All right? That was the reason I sent him up there! *I'm afraid of heights.'* He shouted up at Auden in supplication, 'Phil. Please. For God's sake be careful!' He saw the Acts Of Merit Man smile. Spencer, going red-faced, said with sudden desperation, 'I'm supposed to be the clever one and I haven't got the faintest idea on Earth what he's doing.' He asked the Acts Of Merit Man in genuine, real supplication, 'Please, what the hell is he doing?'

On the roof, Auden yelled in triumph, 'Fish. I can smell fish.' No need for the Acts Of Merit Man to explain. He was about to do it. Auden, nodding, yelled down, 'See, Bill? *Zen Buddhists always hit people.*' He said happily, 'Ha!' He was He Of The Clear Mind. Auden, standing up to his full height, holding the coat out in front of him like a toreador, listening carefully as downstairs in the monastery the monks began chanting, smiling, baring his teeth in triumph, yelled, 'They're being hit now only they don't know it.'

Auden yelled, 'Zen. There isn't much to Zen.'

Auden, roaring like a Colossus, shouted at the top of his voice, 'O.K. RELEASE ALL THE PIGEONS AT ONCE.'

Above the flyover leading from Moore's Pocket away to Central and Kowloon, Chief Inspector Kyle-Foxby said softly to himself, 'Damn it. Damn it.'

It shouldn't be happening. The system had all been planned, computerized, programmed, systematized, ordered to the nth variable – to a point where there were no variables – and it should not be happening.

With three streets off line what he should have been seeing below him was a crush of unmoving vehicles as the feeder roads all backed up and, honking, shouting and cursing, no one in their cars went anywhere.

Hong Kong had the worst traffic problem in the world. He had ameliorated it. He had introduced the perfect system of one way streets and ameliorated it.

Below him, with the three streets out, he should have had to take rapid, pro tem measures with his Traffic policemen and keep the system going at half pace until the streets could be repaired and re-opened.

He had nothing to do. He needed no one. On his radio, he heard the voice of one of his policemen say in that stupid, half English Chinese accent they all had, 'System flowing one hundred per cent perfect. Traffic flow rate eighteen per cent above normal speed,' and Kyle-Foxby, pausing only to clench his fists against the railings of the bridge said evenly back, 'Thank you very much.'

On the bridge above the flyover, Chief Inspector Kyle-Foxby, said, at a total loss to understand, '*Damn it.*'

8

The air was full of pigeons. Wheeling and diving, they were not flying free above the roof as acts of merit, they were flying over the roof for a free feed. At the topmost gargoyle, Auden, sniffing and snorting, yelled, 'See! Satori! Enlightenment!' He was being covered in pigeon dung. The pigeons were not trying to avoid him: they were aiming for him. Auden, crouching down and kissing, embracing one of the gargoyles, yelled, 'See, Bill, see!' He wrenched at the gargoyle and took its head off completely then ducked as six pigeons made a dash to take his fingers. Auden, in ecstasy, yelled, 'See! There isn't much to Zen but you have to have the instinct for it!' He saw the Acts Of Merit Man doubled over in joyous laughter in the courtyard. Auden, bouncing up and down on his size ten shoes on the roof peak that was never intended to hold more than a size one, shrieked down in concert with the laughter, 'I see! I see! Nothing is something. Something is nothing!' He shouted down to Spencer, 'It's a poor monastery! They have no Master! They spend all their time gazing at walls!' He shrieked as a pigeon almost removed one of his ears in its frenzy to get at the gargoyle head, 'Hit! Target!' He pulled the severed head away and held it under his coat. He saw the Acts Of Merit Man holding his stomach and guffawing with laughter. In the laughter there was no sound. Under the long robes, beneath the skull cap and pigtail there was a silence. Like the picture in the book, at last, someone was sitting around being silent. He knew. He *knew*. There wasn't much to Zen Buddhism, but what there was –

Auden, howling with laughter, shrieked down, 'The target the shooter aims at is himself!' He held up the head. 'What is it supposed to be?'

The Acts Of Merit Man, still doubled up, yelled back, '*Heroin!* It's supposed to be heroin!' The Acts Of Merit Man, not looking very worried, yelled up, 'Watch out for the guns!'

There were gun barrels everywhere. They were coming up from every hole in the roof. Auden, glancing at them, yelled back, 'Ha! Ha! Ha!' He wasn't worried. Under his coat, pecking at the severed gargoyle head, he had a pigeon. Auden – a moment before the tapers all hit the touch-holes of the hand cannons and practically blew the roof off its rafters – yelled in ecstasy, 'I Have Seen The Light!'

'Phil –!'

Auden, still cackling, yelled, 'Forget it!' Buddhists never ate meat. They never killed. They stared at walls and wondered. Auden, drawing his enormous Colt Python .357 magnum and holding the pigeon by the neck in his other hand in the coat, said happily, 'Ignoramus, am I? Bloody ignoramus, am I? Smarter than a monastery full of second-rate untutored locally-recruited bloody novice monks!'

Auden, speaking Cantonese, standing on the peak of the roof, thundered out at the top of his voice, 'You in there – all of you – come out with your hands up or –'

He put the giant gun to the head of the squirming bird and held it up.

The sun was behind him above the roof.

In that light, up there, he looked like God.

Auden, standing alone, needing no one, lacking nothing – not even *Guns and Ammo* magazine – thundered out in dire, terrible warning, 'Come out or the bird gets it first!'

Auden, in the finest moment of his life, said in total, complete conquest, 'Heroin – ha! What it is – of course – is *fishpaste*!'

He saw the Acts Of Merit Man smile.

Holding the bird so gently in his hand that it thought it was merely being comforted, Auden, his big red face, like the Acts Of Merit Man's, soft and kindly, without reservation, all his teeth showing, did the same.

Making dynamite was easy. All you had to do was mix glycerine, nitric and sulphuric acid at a zero temperature to make nitroglycerine, then, if you were still alive and the process had been supervised so well that the freezer you made it in hadn't turned into a bomb case and blown you, it and the surrounding neighbourhood to tripes, you soaked the nitro through a clay like kieselguhr, let it dry and – if what you made didn't leak little droplets onto the floor and blow the entire building you made it in down – what you had was dynamite.

In the Bomb Squad laboratory in Aberdeen Street, Technical Inspector Matthews, taking scrapings from plastic bags full of brick and masonry from Sepoy Street, finding clay, said softly to himself, 'Hmm.' There was a thin piece of wire embedded in the clay and, using forceps, he extracted it and laid it out on a piece of stark white paper on his bench.

On the paper, the wire was S-shaped. It was scorched and, at the very end where it had made a connection with a battery or a timing device, it was twisted.

These days, everyone knew how to make bombs. All you had to do was find a military bookshop, go through their lists of ex-Army and Special Forces Improvised Ordnance Manuals until you found the one you wanted, buy yourself a kid's printing set so you could make up a letterhead stating you ran a private museum or were a bona fide military historian, order the damned thing, and the bookseller, having complied with the law designed to keep bomb-making manuals out of the hands of bomb-makers, would be delighted to send it to you, post paid.

Mind you, that was only if you were a private bomb-maker. If you were a genuine terrorist you could simply buy The Anarchist's Cook Book.

If you were the studious type you could simply take a degree in chemistry.

Detonators were even easier. All you needed for one of them was a piece of low resistance wire, or, if you were making some sort of hand grenade or anti-personnel trip-wire gun, a single percussion cap for a muzzle-loading gun, or, if you couldn't get one of those – and you usually could – a cap from a child's toy pistol.

Everyone knew how to make bombs. In the laboratory, flicking on a strong neon light above the square of white paper, Technical Inspector Matthews, wiping his hands on his dirty dust coat, bent down to look closely at the wire. What they didn't know – the amateurs, the professionals, all of them – was that each of the bombs they made, because of the way they made it, had a special, unique, distinct signature. Looking at even the way the wire was twisted could tell an expert not only how the bomb was made, but where – in all those books and sources – the bomber had got the information on how to make it.

There was not as much wire as Matthews would have liked for a full examination, but, like the bombers themselves, he had to work with what he could get.

Moving his desk glass over to cover the paper and clicking it up to fifty magnifications, Matthews looked carefully at the length of twisted wire with the eye, not of a self-taught, but of a professional, knowledgeable expert.

On the phone in the Detectives' Room, Arthur Collins from the Main Roads Department said evenly, 'I'm in a bar in Wanchai Street – a dirty little dive called Alice's that serves strong liquor in bloody dark corners – and what I'm doing is getting drunk.' On the phone, his Scottish accent was very pronounced. Collins, his voice punctuated by tinkling sounds as in Alice's other people also got drunk, said with a slur in his voice, 'I'm getting drunk because I haven't got anyone at home I want to go to and I'm forty-eight years old and I retire in two years and I haven't got the faintest idea what I'm going to do for a living when I do.' Behind his voice, the tinkling turned into a crash as someone, presumably well in his cups, knocked over a something he must have been building on a table with his empty glasses. Collins, dropping his voice, said slowly, 'And also because I've never seen a dead person before today and today, in Sepoy Street, I saw all the dead people I ever want to see for the rest of my life.' There was no force in his voice: with the booze it sounded weak and undirected. Collins, drawing a deep breath to muster his thoughts, said spitefully, 'I saw you there. You've seen a hell of a lot of dead bodies – it's what you cops do – and I couldn't think of anyone else to talk to who I knew had seen the same thing I saw and –' He was wandering, '– and who it didn't affect.' He stopped with the sound of the bar behind him, 'Do you follow?'

At his desk, looking down at the open file in front of him, Feiffer said into the phone, 'I suppose so –'

'I know everybody thinks all we bloody Scotsmen do nothing but sit around getting pissed –' He put on his Robbie Burns voice, '– sipping wee drams an' all that, ye ken – and thinking about the bloody mist and the heather, but this is one Scotsman –' He stopped. He said suddenly, 'I saw you there. I've never seen a dead person before and I didn't know who else to talk to.' He was feeling sorry for himself. Collins said, 'I wanted to talk to someone.'

He had found a single black Shensi-embroidered slipper. One of the photographers had taken a picture of it. Looking up, Feiffer asked quietly, 'How long will the street be out of commission?'

'Sepoy Street?' He made a hiccoughing sound. 'Sepoy? For bloody ever. Weeks – how the hell do I know? A long time.' He seemed to be trying to say something else, but the words would not form themselves clearly in his mind, 'First the electricity people have got to do their work with the road up, then the telephone company – with the road still up – then – then –' Collins said, 'I don't know: a whole lot of people – and then Main Roads, finally, at last, gets to work on it and before we even think about fixing up the road we have to tear it open to see how much we have to fix.' He seemed to be losing concentration fast, 'I don't know – maybe the road'll never be fixed and they can just close it off and use it as a bloody bowling alley!' There was the tinkling sound again, and then the laughter of the one of the hostesses. Collins said bitterly, 'You're used to it, all this death and –' He said to someone with sudden vehemence, 'Shut up.' He was sighing deeply, trying to get his breath and clear his head, 'I'm like all bloody wandering Scotsmen: all I want to do is make my fortune so I can retire to the exact same bloody damp, miserable, fog-blown, blasted bit of the bloody Highlands or the Lowlands that, when I was a young man, I spent my entire time trying to escape.' He said bitterly, 'Some hope.' His voice was fading away, 'Some bloody, forlorn, pitiable, forlorn bloody hope that.' Collins said abruptly, 'I'm sorry I bothered you, but I couldn't think of anyone else to ring.'

'That's all right.'

'Those – those other people in the street: the ones – the ones who were screaming – some of them have died too now, haven't they?'

'Yes.'

'I'm in a bar at 2.15 in the afternoon on a bloody working day with my retirement coming up in two years – for a bloody Scotsman that's not canny, is it?' The Robbie Burns accent was meant to provoke. He had obviously used it a lot. Collins, thickening it even further, said, 'Well, is it? Och, man, d'ye ken what I'm saying? Och, aye . . .'

Feiffer said softly, 'Why don't you finish your drink and go home?'

'*Home?*' The accent was gone, the voice bitter and hard. 'Home?' Collins, all the traces of alcohol gone momentarily from his voice, said in impotent fury, 'Where's that? Where I can forget about what I saw today, where I can go back to living in a dirty little two up, two down semi-detached in Glasgow where I grew up? Where I can live like a laird on my bloody Hong Kong wandering Scotsman bloody pension?' Collins said, 'Some hope. Some forlorn hope.'

He had worked himself up to anger. With the sounds of the bar at 2.15 p.m. loud behind him, Collins, a man totally out of place, shouted down the line with real hatred, 'You rotten, lousy bastard – it's all right for people like you – you're all bloody used to it all – *aren't you?*'

In the courtyard, the sand gardener, collecting the sixteen Ming dynasty hand cannons from each of the Ming dynasty hand cannon carrying novices, said sadly in Cantonese, 'We are a poor order. In the cruel world of capitalism, unless our Master comes to join us from China, we will have nothing.' He looked at the severed gargoyle head in Auden's hand. The severed gargoyle's head smelled of moulded, dried-out fish paste. The sand gardener gazing at the Acts Of Merit Man's re-caged pigeons, said sincerely, 'We would not have hurt your pigeons. We aimed away.' He glanced up at the roof. It was still smoking. The sand gardener, explaining all, said, 'We were told by letter from our Master in China that it was heroin to insure the financial future of the monastery.'

The Enlightened Man Spoke Seldom. In the courtyard, Auden, nodding, said, 'Hmm.' He looked at the hand cannons. He looked at Spencer. The Totally Stunned Man was Also Silent. From Spencer there was not even an 'Oh.' Auden, sighing, said, 'Ah.'

The sand gardener, staring at the ground, said softly, 'We could not kill the pigeons because of our beliefs. You knew that.' He looked broken. 'In every way we have spent our time in fruitless endeavour protecting a future that was never there.' He looked at Auden for confirmation.

Auden said, 'Hmm.' Funny, but for the first time in his life, although he had things to say, he wanted to say nothing. Auden, glancing at the Acts Of Merit Man, nodded.

The sand gardener, looking desperate, said sadly, 'We need our Master.'

Auden said, 'Hmm.'

In an undertone, Spencer said softly in English, 'Phil, I – I'm just amazed . . .'

'Hmm.' He looked and saw the Acts Of Merit Man's old, kindly face staring at him. Auden, speaking Cantonese, said quietly to the sand gardener, 'You must wait until your Master needs you.' He smiled. Zen Buddhists spent their time going around hitting people. The novices were being hit. Only, so far, it had not hurt.

Auden, taking Spencer gently by the arm and beginning to lead him towards the monastery door to the street, said softly to The Acts Of Merit Man in English as he passed, 'Master, the next time, for their lesson, please choose something a little less violent.' He saw Spencer look amazed. Auden, patting him mercifully on the shoulder, said softly, 'I read a book once.' He patted Spencer a little harder on the shoulder to reassure him.

Auden said encouragingly, 'It was about Zen Buddhism and self-knowledge, but to tell you the truth, Bill, I never did finish it.'

It was almost another two weeks until *Guns and Ammo* got to the Colony. Auden said with genuine curiosity, 'I never knew you were afraid of heights.' It was something one friend really should know about another.

Auden asked kindly, 'Anything I can do to help?'

In the Detectives' Room, it was 5 p.m. Feiffer, at his desk, watching O'Yee on all fours feeding the dog beef and cashew nuts from a take-away on the floor, said with concern, 'Christopher, you are going to eat tonight, aren't you? Yourself?' The dog was making slurping noises. It liked the beef but hated the nuts. O'Yee was separating them for it with chopsticks.

O'Yee said, 'Sure.' The dog wasn't too keen on the sauce either. O'Yee moved it out of the way with the chopsticks, 'Of course I am.'

'You can come home with me.' The file of photographs was on Feiffer's desk. He didn't look at it. 'Nicola will be only too delighted and if —' The file was closed. He had his hand resting on it. 'Or we can go out to eat. There's a place in Kowloon that we've been to before, in Nathan Road —' He saw O'Yee glance up for a moment. 'What do you say?'

'What about the dog?'

'The dog'll be O.K. here. We can ask the Night Sergeant to put it in one of the cells or –'

'No. No, I'd feel stupid coming back here at midnight bailing out a bloody dog.' He found a particularly succulent piece of beef and shoved it in the dog's direction. O'Yee, shaking his head, said, 'No, thanks all the same Harry –'

'You don't have to come back here. We've got a spare bed –'

'No, no thanks.' The dog looked up. O'Yee patted it reassuringly. O'Yee said, smiling, 'No, no, thanks, Harry, it's good of you, but really –'

'How long before Emily and the kids are due back?'

'Soon.' O'Yee, not looking up, said nodding, 'Oh, soon enough. You know . . .' Outside it was 5 p.m. You could hear the rush hour traffic starting. In an hour or two it would be dark. O'Yee, still patting, said off-handedly, 'Thanks anyway.' Soon it would be dark and silent. O'Yee, brightening, said, 'Um – what sort of dog do you think it is, Harry?'

'I think it's a pretty good dog.' The file was on Feiffer's desk. Outside, soon, it would be dark. Feiffer put his hand on the file and, for a moment, felt afraid. 'I don't know. I speak a little Szechuan dialect – do you want me to try a few words of that on it?'

'No.' O'Yee, shaking his head, said pleasantly, 'No, thanks all the same.' He thought of a night in a tiny, lonely cell in the lockup.

O'Yee, smiling, said, 'No, thanks all the same, Harry. Maybe tomorrow.' He patted the dog encouragingly as the dog went on eating the separated bits of meat. 'I think I'll keep him with me tonight.' He said with sudden vehemence, 'Poor bastard, he looks like he hasn't had a good meal for bloody days.'

'O.K.' Outside, soon, it would be dark.

In Sepoy Street, he had found a single black, embroidered slipper. The embroidery was from Shensi province. They would never know who had owned it.

Feiffer, putting the file in the top drawer of his desk and

locking it up, said, nodding, 'O.K., fine. Whatever you like.'

It was time to go home. Somehow, although he wanted to do it very much, he could not bring himself to leave.

. . . Small boys stone frogs to death for sport,
But frogs do not die for sport; they die in earnest.

At 5 p.m. unable to shake a feeling of real, terrible dread, Feiffer, silently, sat watching O'Yee hand-feeding the dog.

It was gone, wasted. At his window on the third floor of the Department Of Urban Development on Wyang Street, Albert Nonte, smoking a cigarette, considered the course of his life. It was gone, wasted, all – all the hopes and aspirations and plans – all gone for nothing. The Great Dream: the new course of American foreign policy, A.B.s, M.A.s, Ph.D.s: all, all totally and finally, gone for nothing.

He was the only man – probably in the world – who had a working, colloquial command of six Chinese dialects and major languages and now, naming streets, studying yellowed, meaningless records from a Colony going nowhere, it had all been for nothing.

At his window, Nonte said softly, 'China.' It wasn't China, it was Hong Kong. It was a conquest from an Opium War fought a hundred years ago and, when the Chinese felt like it, they were going to take it back and turn it into – probably – nothing more than a bone and guts dump for the Canton fishing fleet or a sump for the discharges from their oil tankers.

The Colony had come from nowhere and it was going nowhere. It was the last vestige of an Empire that had been born in the nineteenth century and progressed from that intellectual, colonial and moral position not at all.

Below him, he could see the traffic building up for the rush hour. Hong Kong was an island: in a car, on foot, any way you tried it, there was nowhere to go.

Nonte, beyond tears, said with a sick feeling in his stomach he carried with him all the time, *'Ch'i jen t'ien hsiang.'* It meant, 'Heaven stands by the good man.' It was from the

Classical Examination the Emperors had held in China for a thousand years and now, with no Emperors, an examination that was held no longer.

Hong Kong.

There was nowhere else for him to go.

Toponomy: the naming of streets.

At his window, he looked out at those streets of Hong Kong and hated them.

It was a signature. On every bit of work, no matter how small, there was always the signature of the man who did it. In his basement laboratory, Technical Inspector Matthews, holding the tiny piece of wire from the Sepoy Street bomb between his fingers, said softly to himself, 'Yeah.'

Under the glass, he had seen the way the bomber had used his watchmaker's pliers to strip the wire to make a connection, then, uniquely, unknowingly, automatically, given it a double twist back on itself and then, turning the pliers in his hand, twisted it back the other way again.

He had done it totally without being aware of it: while he talked to someone standing next to him or while his mind was on something else – he had done it, not been aware of it, and then, not even knowing he had done it, set about connecting it up to whatever part of the bomb it fitted into.

Standing at his bench, gazing along the rows of grenades and devices set up for study and inspiration on the walls of the place, Matthews tried to think where he had seen a signature like that before.

It was a professional bomb-maker's job. There were no professional bomb-makers.

He glanced at his watch. He had been standing there, gazing at the wire and thinking about it, for over two hours.

Unknowingly, his mind on something else, Matthews, playing with the other end of the wire, gave it a double twist back on itself and then, turning his fingers to get at it, twisted it back the other way again.

It was a signature.

It was his own.
Outside, it was almost 5.08 p.m.
It was almost the end of the first day.
Outside, in the streets, it was almost night.

9

He knew roads. He knew roads and streets and highways and flyovers and systems: he knew all of it – he knew the theory and the practice.

In his Police Land Rover at 1 a.m., parked on Hong Bay Beach Road watching the lights of the fishing boats, Chief Inspector Kyle-Foxby, in full uniform, said softly, 'I know every inch of it.' He had studied it, learned it, designed the one way street system that made it all work. He knew all the statistics: 618.21 miles of road in the Colony of which 204.10 were on the island, 182.06 on Kowloon, and in the New Territories: fast becoming not a rural hinterland for the Colony but itself another giant non stop highway, 232.05.

It did him no good at all. He knew nothing. Isandula Street: 0.21 of a mile, General Gordon Street, 0.2 exactly of a mile and Sepoy Street –

He had designed the one way system they were part of.

The system should have collapsed.

He knew all the statistics and all the theory and all the practice – and he knew nothing and the traffic had not stopped but went on as if neither he nor the streets had ever existed.

1 a.m. Wiping his gloved hand gently across his eyes, Chief Inspector Kyle-Foxby started the engine of his vehicle and gently backed it out into the street, being careful to glance both ways to make sure the manoeuvre was safe.

Hong Bay Beach Road was deserted. As he reversed, for a moment, he saw his own headlamps reflected in the water in front of him.

He knew roads. He knew roads and streets and highways and flyovers and systems. He knew all of it – he knew the theory and the practice.

Somewhere – now – something was happening to all his roads and streets and flyovers. Something was happening to him.

He knew it.

Somewhere, somehow, they were out there.

He knew traffic. He knew nothing about people at all.

Proceeding carefully towards Canton Street, at the regulation maximum night time speed laid down by law, he flicked his indicator lever on to signal a turn.

It was the third time in the last two hours he had travelled over the route.

Driving slowly through the streets, seeing people everywhere, with an effort of will, he tried to make out, in the light of the street lamps, what they were all doing.

He understood people. He knew what made them tick. In the main room of the third floor apartment on Singapore Road, the man of limited time, working by flashlight, went directly to the roll-top desk by the window and began going through its drawers.

The feeling he had had all day still niggled at him. He knew he would not feel happy until he had settled it. The drawers contained, as he had expected, the accumulated debris of a neat mind: paperclips in boxes, bulldog clips in little glass bowls, pens, sharpened pencils, and stamped envelopes arranged in piles for local or airmail.

He nodded to himself. He was wrong. He had seen something in Sepoy Street, drawn the wrong conclusions, and he was wrong.

There was a photograph of the two occupants of the apartment on top of the desk. With his gloved hand he took it up for a moment and looked at it with something approaching affection. He had been wrong. He pulled open the last drawer in the desk and, nodding, saw that it contained nothing more than the normal household papers and receipts one would expect to find anywhere.

There was not even a lock on the desk: there was nothing there – or in the entire apartment – to worry about. The man of limited time, feeling relieved, flicked back his head and ran his gloved fingers through his hair to settle it. It was a strangely feminine gesture, but at night, alone in the apartment, satisfied, he felt free to do it.

Sliding the roll top down on the desk and glancing again at the photograph in the faint light from his flashlight, the man of limited time was pleased to be wrong.

Behind him, in the centre of the room, he could see a blinking yellow light as the answer machine on the telephone recorded a message and he thought for a moment of waiting until it was finished to play it back to see who it was.

The niggling feeling was gone. There was nothing to worry about.

The telephone had a whistle playback activator which meant he could listen to the message being recorded from any telephone anywhere. Flicking for a second time at his hair, the man of limited time thought that he would do it a little later in Khartoum Street.

It was six minutes past 1 a.m.

He had other, more important things to do first.

Pausing only momentarily to glance at the flashing light as whoever it was on the other end of the line recorded his message, and slip the whistle into his pocket, the man of limited time, making no sound at all, went quickly to the front door of the apartment and, using his key, let himself out.

It was hopeless: totally, utterly hopeless. It wasn't what he had been trained for. He had been trained for Traffic, for administration, for a career, and in the middle of the night, driving around and around along the same route looking at people, he was getting nowhere at all.

Pausing for a moment at a Give Way sign at the bottom of Singapore Road and applying the handbrake, Chief Inspector Kyle-Foxby, staring at the knot of people lining the road – at the brothel area that started at the west end of Yellowthread Street and continued up into Hanford Hill – ran his hand across his hair and said firmly, 'No.'

It wasn't what he had been trained for. There were people standing around arguing and bartering, shouting at each other and gesticulating – he had no idea whether it was in anger or fun, or whether –

Kyle-Foxby said firmly, 'No.' It wasn't what he had been trained for.

People like Feiffer – people like the cop in the ambulance with Lo – they were the people who did this sort of thing: the dinosaurs of police work – the men with local knowledge, cops going nowhere, content in their work, seedy and –

He saw someone in the crowd of people raise his fist and his hand went for the door handle, but it was only some sort of gesture as part of the story the man was evidently telling his friends. At the gesture the crowd around the man began laughing uproariously.

He knew Traffic. That was where his career was leading, one planned, organized, systematic move at a time.

He didn't even speak fluent Cantonese. He had planned to be in the Colony a maximum of five years and, to organize a new Traffic system – to cover yourself in administrative glory in the midst of the worst street network in the world – all you needed was to be able to talk to a computer.

It was what he had been trained to do – what he wanted.

In the streets at night, driving around and around in circles, Chief Inspector Kyle-Foxby, watching people, stared out through the windscreen of his Police Land Rover into the faces of all the people on the streets and, not having been trained for it, had no idea at all what any of them were thinking.

*

It niggled at him. It had done for some hours.

In his apartment, Feiffer, sitting on the edge of the bed, stared at the mute telephone in his hand and wondered.

He hated talking to answering machines. Even after using them for years he still had an automatic urge to say goodbye to the thing a moment before, at the end of the message-taking, with an unemotional click, they cut him off.

It was past 1 a.m.: too late to have rung anyway.

It niggled at him.

Something about it niggled at him.

Hearing his wife coming in from the other room ready for bed, Feiffer put the receiver back on its cradle and tried to put it from his mind.

It niggled at him.

He thought for a moment of trying to ring again.

It was the night. At night, in the silence, things always assumed too much importance.

It was nothing, just a feeling.

It was eight minutes past 1 a.m. in the morning, and he could not shake the feeling that, somehow, then, at that moment, he should have done something more than simply leave a message.

Someone had even told him the man Feiffer spoke three or four Chinese dialects. Well, that was him and if he had his future tied up in a Colony that was going to die like every other Colony had died in the last hundred years then that was his problem.

In his Land Rover, drawing up to the intersection of Yellow-thread Street and Empress Of India Street, Chief Inspector Kyle-Foxby, feeling angry, looked both ways and then, changing down, went at the regulation speed towards Khartoum Street, the one-way system he had designed, and the flyover he had been in part responsible for urging, towards the Police Barracks in Central and home.

It wasn't what he had been trained for and there were plenty of people around like Feiffer with his gun and his crumpled clothing and his vast, great, clever knowledge of people who could do it better.

He knew Traffic! That was where the future lay and anyone who claimed that in the long run the car should not be allowed to take over from people simply hadn't thought about the problem and, if they had – and he had heard plenty of them at dinner parties, half cut and full of opinions – they were totally unable to come up with an alternative.

There was no alternative.

He had made the right decision.

The future lay in exactly the field he had chosen to be in. He was not a *cop*, he was a police officer. There was a difference. Twenty minutes past 1 a.m. For the last two and a quarter hours he had been totally wasting his time.

Passing the four ways at Khartoum Street and East Yellow-thread Street, Kyle-Foxby, speaking in a whisper, said with vehemence, 'Fuck him!' He knew people like Feiffer. That was the way they talked. Clenching the wheel, Kyle-Foxby said again, 'Fuck you! What the hell do you know about anything?' He glanced in the mirror and saw people waiting at the lights on the four ways, legally, one man on each corner, waiting for the lights to change – in an ordered, systematic fashion – in a fashion he had designed.

He knew Traffic. Whatever some group of lunatics was doing to the streets had nothing to do with what he did – it had to do with people like Feiffer.

Outside the ambulance in General Gordon Street, with all his education and knowledge, he had felt like a fool. He saw, in the rear view mirror, someone cross Khartoum Street to go towards a telephone booth. At the lights the four men were still waiting to cross. He knew Traffic. He knew –

Kyle-Foxby said in a gasp, 'God Almighty.'

He knew Traffic.

He knew Traffic and he knew that all four traffic lights did not register *STOP* at once. He saw, dimly in the reflected light in his mirror, one of the men bend down with something in his hand.

He saw the man on the other corner raise his arm and wave to the first man. He saw —

He saw the lights changing through green, amber to red, and back again. He saw that not one of the four men went to cross.

He saw —

He was in the middle of a one way street. There was no one around. He could have made a U-turn to reach them, but it was illegal.

Feeling the sweat standing out on his forehead, Chief Inspector Kyle-Foxby, obeying the rules he himself had set down, accelerated away down the street to make a left turn legally to bring him back to the intersection.

It cost him an extra minute and a half exactly more than the U-turn would have cost.

Even with the siren blaring to clear his way, it was an extra minute and a half he did not have to spend.

'. . . *this is Detective Chief Inspector Feiffer. Earlier today when we spoke on the phone . . .*'

In the telephone booth on Khartoum Street, the man of limited time, his eyes widening, froze at the receiver. The recorded words were unhurried, bland, familiar . . .

'. . . *talk further about . . .*'

The man of limited time still had the whistle out to signal up the answering machine. It seemed to be glowing hot in his gloved hand.

Down the street at the four ways he could see his people at the traffic signals. For an instant he thought he heard —

It was a siren.

Almost dropping the whistle in his haste to get out of the booth, the man of limited time, running for his car, shouted down the length of the street to the four ways, 'Back! Back to the car!' The man of limited time, shouting at the top of his voice in Chinese, shrieked, '*Run.*'

In the Land Rover, turning hard to make the corner to get back onto East Yellowthread Street, Kyle-Foxby saw them start to move. They were shadows, four of them, they seemed to be trying to get up from something they were doing at the bottom of the traffic lights. In the street itself there was another shadow at a car waving and shouting. He saw three of the shadows at the lights turn and start towards him, the fourth, pausing, stopping, behind the others, maybe not understanding what was going on. On the cab of the Land Rover the siren was blaring at top volume, all the lights on the roof blinking and flashing. The lights facing him were all GO: there was nothing going to stop him getting into Khartoum Street.

At the far end of the street the man at the car seemed to disappear for a moment and then reappear again. He was a silhouette, a shadow. There was something in his hand. Kyle-Foxby, wrenching the microphone from the dashboard, shouted into the radio above the siren, 'Chief Inspector's car Khartoum and East Yellowthread Streets! Incident in progress!' He heard static from the radio and then, above the siren, a garbled transmission. He had the vehicle at full speed, the wheels spinning on the roadway as he turned into East Yellowthread Street. 'Assistance required! Repeat, assistance required!' He was racing, pushing the motor to full power. He saw the three men at the lights running, the fourth, older, slower, a little behind them. There was no more speed to be got out of the Land Rover. He heard the engine shriek in protest. With the button pushed down hard, slicing through any replies Base might be able to make, Kyle-Foxby yelled above the siren, '*Now*. I want assistance *now!*'

He saw him. He saw him pause at the traffic lights. In the middle of the street, the man of limited time, wrenching his sawn off riot gun from the back seat, screamed at the three men running at him, 'It was him. He talked to the law. It was him.' He heard the siren and then, reflected off the buildings and in the night sky, he saw the flashing light. The traitor was still at the traffic light, stumbling, still holding something in his hand. The man of limited time, getting the gun up to his shoulder and working the action to get a shell into the breech, yelled, 'I trusted you!' It was only going to take one shot. It didn't matter where it went. Coming towards him, stumbling, too old for the job, too weak, too stupid, too soft, he saw the traitor with the device still in his hand. The road was clear. He heard the siren coming. The man of limited time, taking aim, not at the stumbling man, but at the side of a building, yelled in English at the top of his voice, *'You lied to me!'*

He saw the flash. In his Land Rover as he turned he saw the flash. In the cab Kyle-Foxby said in involuntary terror, 'Jesus!' He actually saw the weapon kick against the man's shoulder and identified it: a Winchester 1400. He saw the shell fly out of the ejection port and then, as the shot struck the side of a building, sparks fly off into the roadway. Half way down the street, the three men were clambering into the car, fighting each other in their terror to get away. He saw the last man – older, slower – seem to stop in the roadway and then turn with something in his hand – a tobacco box or a slab of metal, something that glittered in the light as the traffic signals changed. He saw –

He knew him. For a moment, as he turned, he knew who it was. He saw him hold the tobacco box as some sort of trophy or –

He was trying to get rid of it. In that instant he was trying to get rid of it, but it was somehow stuck fast in his hand and he was trying to get rid of it and he couldn't find anywhere to put it down. He saw the man open his mouth to shout something and he knew, in that same instant, that it was a bomb. There were more of them stuck on the bases of all the pylons and in that instant as the bomb in the stumbling man's hand and all the bombs on the pylons of the traffic lights went off, Kyle-Foxby, swallowed up by fire and a concussion that turned his vehicle over in the street, yelled hopelessly, 'No! Not here! Not *here*!'

He knew Traffic. He knew nothing about people at all, not even himself, and, lying caught in his seat belt in the wrecked Land Rover on its side in the middle of the street, for what seemed like a very long time he thought, with tears streaming down his face, that there, in that awful place, for no good reason at all, inconsequentially, he had been killed.

1.27 a.m. In the car, speeding away, the man of limited time shouted back from the wheel, 'It can't be me! How can it be me? You! You have to be the one to do it!' He was still gasping with effort and his voice would not come strongly enough for him to be heard over the sound of the engine. He could see the faces of the three of them in the back seat, their eyes wide and staring. There was a single European between the two Chinese in the back seat. He had to be the one. It was up to him.

The man of limited time, reaching Empress Of India Street and trying to slow down for the traffic, put his fist to his head to wipe away the sweat. He was still wearing gloves. He saw his hand shaking.

The man of limited time, forcing himself to be calm, said tightly in Chinese, 'Right? It has to be you. You have to be the one to do it!'

He got no reaction. He was in the main stream of traffic. There were cars and people everywhere.

The man of limited time shrieked, 'It has to be! It has to be you!'

He saw, in the back, the man close his eyes for a moment and nod. Everywhere in the vehicle, there was the stink of sweat. The man of limited time said, 'Right.' He felt his hands stop shaking.

The man of limited time, driving slowly, calming, said evenly to the other passengers in the car, 'Right?'

1.28 a.m.

Clicking on the indicator on the column of his steering wheel to signal his intention, the man of limited time turned the car into Jade Road to join the one way system to travel north.

10

It was Arthur Collins. It was what was left of him. The bomb he had been holding had gone off at chest height like a Claymore mine and, like a Claymore, it had killed him by the uncomplicated, sure and simple method of cutting him in half. Bending down over the torso and head with Feiffer in the middle of the cordoned-off street, the Government Medical Officer, Doctor Macarthur, glancing up momentarily to where the police tow truck was winching the capsized Land Rover back up onto its wheels, said softly, 'Blast effect. Some minor shrapnel from what was fairly obviously a small metal container holding the charge, but almost all the damage is classical blast injury.' The head appeared intact. He put his surgical gloved hand gently onto the temple and moved it and it wasn't intact at all. Macarthur, bending close down to the remains of the chest cavity and moving the head back and forth to get a better view of it in the early dawn light, glanced up for a moment to where Matthews from the Bomb Squad shouted an order to the tow truck crew to clear the area so he could get at the three blown down traffic lights. Macarthur, looking, as always in the presence of the remains of a human being, fascinated by the intricacies of the method which had destroyed it, said with interest, 'It's a shredding wound. Death by massive traumatic insult.' He looked up. He put his fingers somewhere inside what was left of the chest, he felt at the lungs. 'Leaving aside the amputation of the legs and the pelvic region, there probably isn't a single organ or piece of viscera that hasn't been completely torn to pieces.' He took his hand out of the chest and, his gloved fingers bloody, touched at the side of the head again. Macarthur, in his own little world, not looking up at Feiffer's face, asked with genuine curiosity, 'Who did you say he was?'

Above him, Chief Inspector Kyle-Foxby said firmly, 'Arthur Collins from the Department Of Main Roads.' He was not going to look away this time. He knew Feiffer was watching. Kyle-Foxby, touching at his sole injury, a surface abrasion on the left side of his face, said above the noise of the tow truck winch, 'I recognized him when he turned around to see me.' He was standing above Macarthur, looking down into Feiffer's face. 'I was on off-duty patrol, checking the streets and when I became aware of something out of the ordinary I investigated and, proceeding down –' He saw Feiffer look away towards the traffic lights '– and proceeding in this direction, seeing four men running away I became suspicious and I – I was too late to –' Feiffer turned to watch Matthews at the downed traffic lights. Matthews was on his hands and knees scraping at the roadway with a spatula. '– and I –' Feiffer's hands were clean. So far, he had not laid a single finger on the body. '– and I –' Kyle-Foxby, feeling slighted, demanded, 'Aren't you going to search him? There was a man here with a shotgun! It was only pure luck he didn't put a charge in through my windscreen and I'd be lying here dead too!' He saw Feiffer purse his lips. He was still looking away. Kyle-Foxby, brushing at his uniform and then touching quickly at the abrasion on his face, demanded, 'Well?'

'What the hell did you think you were doing here?'

'I was trying to stop a crime!'

'I see. Did you call for assistance?'

'Yes, I called for assistance! I called for assistance the moment I realized that there was a man with a gun and people were setting off bombs in the street!' He couldn't understand why Feiffer was not going to touch the body. It was like a dead rabbit: if someone else had shot it, you weren't aware of the blood and the mess; if it was your own then you were interested. Kyle-Foxby, moving Macarthur out of the way and leaning down with his hand outstretched to touch the face, said, irritated at the slowness of the procedure, 'What you should do while you're still on the scene –'

'Don't touch him!' His eyes met Kyle-Foxby's. Feiffer on his knees, looking up, said in a voice full of menace, 'Just don't you touch anything!' Macarthur had his hand on Collins' temple again. He was moving the neck back and forth checking for breaks in the spinal cord. Fciffer, his eyes blazing, said with an effort at control, 'You've done more than enough for one night! So leave it to the people who know what they're doing!'

'What I've done tonight is find your bombers! Which is more than you've done so far.' Kyle-Foxby, tightening his voice so neither the tow truck crew nor Matthews would hear him said, shaking, 'What I've done –' He saw the look on Feiffer's face and didn't care for it, 'I did exactly what the regulations say I should have done! Once I realized there was a crime in progress I proceeded –'

'You came in here like bloody Roy Rogers!' Feiffer, starting to rise and then thinking better of it, said shaking, 'What you did, for all I know, was bloody well cause the incident!'

'There were four of them at the traffic lights with objects in their hands! What was obviously going to happen was –'

'What *did* happen was that someone was killed!'

'Are you seriously telling me that it was my fault?'

'I don't know.' The spinal cord was gone. Macarthur moved the head an extra millimetre and there was the sound of splintered bones grinding against each other. 'I don't know! Do you?' Feiffer, standing up, said, 'All right? Do you know? Do you have any idea what actually happened in the bloody Indian camp here before your one-man Eighth Cavalry started blowing their sirens and flashing their bloody lights?' At the down traffic signals, Technical Inspector Matthews had stopped to listen. He seemed to be grinning. Feiffer shouted above the din as the tow truck men had another longer go at the Land

115

Rover with the winch, 'All right! You were on the spot! You did everything the regulations say you should have done! You saw it all happen! O.K. Fine! At last, a trained witness! You saw them all – *so give me a description of them all!*'

'It was too dark! All I saw was Collins and the man with the gun!' Kyle-Foxby, stepping back a pace, said, shaking his head, 'It was a Winchester 1400 semi automatic 12 gauge shotgun! I saw the shell fly out of the hole on the side!' He nodded to where the Fingerprint Squad were bending down over the shell on the sidewalk dusting it for fingerprints.

'Because that's what shells do in Winchester 1400 semi automatic 12 gauge shotguns?'

'That's right!'

'That's what shells do in any sort of bloody automatic shotgun!' Feiffer, unable to stop, shouted at the man, 'The only reason you thought it was a bloody Winchester was that a bloody Winchester is the only sort of goddamned shotgun you've ever seen! And that was on Day One at the bloody police defensive shooting course in your bloody bright-eyed cadet days! Wasn't it?'

'I don't claim to be any sort of expert on guns!'

'Then what about the car?'

'What car?'

'The car the bloody man with the shotgun was driving! The bloody car the so-called Winchester 1400 and all the rest of it came out of! He wasn't strolling up and down the street carrying it under his arm, was he? Like some sort of terribly, actually, awfully, dontcha know grouse shoot – *was he?*' Feiffer, trembling with the effort, said in a tight voice, 'I'm not going to search the body in the street here because all the body isn't in one piece! I have to wait until it gets to a bloody steel tray in the Morgue and Doctor Macarthur here puts it all together a little bit – that's why I'm not searching the body!' Even after turning over a Land Rover, every one of Kyle-Foxby's uniform buttons were still in place – sewn on, no doubt, with unbreakable, regulation number nine thread – Feiffer, wanting to walk away, but unable to, said with disgust in his voice, 'All right? Does that suit you? Is that in accord with your view of bloody police work?' He had been there. He had got nothing. The half-blind Embarrassment Man in Isandula Street had seen more. Feiffer, clenching his fist against his side, said in what came out as almost a whisper, 'Did you even think to get the licence number of the car?'

'He was in the phone booth. He just went to the car for a second to –' Kyle-Foxby said softly, swallowing '– to get the gun.'

'He didn't shoot at you. He shot into the air to set the bombs off.' On the ground, Collins was meat, nothing more. It was a little after dawn: the start of the second day. Feiffer, putting his hand briefly to his face to find somewhere else to look, not caring if anyone heard or, if they did, what they thought, shouted above the sound of the winch, 'You goddamned, stupid, well-dressed ponce – *you don't even carry a gun!*'

There was nowhere else to look. There was only Collins. Collins was nothing more than meat.

Feiffer, having to walk away, opening and closing his hands, finding nothing else to do with them, said to everything: to the street, to the day, to everything, 'Damn you! God bloody *damn* you!'

'*Police!*'
In the third floor corridor of the apartments on Singapore Road, Spencer, going to the next door in the line and banging on it with his fist, called out in Cantonese, 'This is the Police! All we want is your assistance! There's nothing wrong – open your door, please!' He looked at Auden outside the door to Collins' apartment and shook his head. It was 5.45 a.m., light. Spencer, moving to the next door and pressing on the door bell, called out, 'There's nothing wrong! This is the police! We just want to locate the caretaker so we can get into one of the apartments.' The name on the door said *KWAN* in Chinese characters. Spencer, raising his voice, called out in Cantonese, '*Fie dee lie* – come on now!'

'*Zheng-taam brou* – Criminal Investigation Department.'

Auden, also getting nowhere at his door, called out in English, 'Open up! There's nothing to worry about!' He put his ear to the door. '*Dhuk-caat – zheng-taam-brou!* Open this damned door!'

There was no one. It was as if every flat on the entire floor was vacant. It wasn't. There were cooking smells.

COLLINS. Behind the door, there was not a sound.

Spencer, chewing on his lip, asked, 'What do you think?' It was 5.45 a.m. He looked at his watch and listened for sounds.

Auden, shaking his head, said, 'I don't know.' It was too quiet by half. There should have been someone around. Auden, taking a coin from his pocket, asked, also listening for sounds, 'Heads or tails?' He flipped the coin.

'Heads.'

There was not a single, solitary sound from any of the apartments on the entire floor. There were people there. It was 5.45 a.m. and they could both smell cooking.

Auden, laying the coin on his wrist and uncovering it, said softly, 'Heads.' There was not a single sound from any of the apartments. It was as if, inside, people were cowering in silent terror.

COLLINS . . .

Drawing his Python from its shoulder holster and holding it above his head in both hands, Auden said softly, 'O.K.' He saw Spencer pull his Detective Special from its belt holster and thumb back the hammer. There was something terribly wrong. There was not a sound anywhere.

He heard the sudden, splintering crash as Spencer put his shoulder to the door and broke it down and, dropping to one knee, Auden swung the long barrelled Python directly into the darkened silent room behind him to cover him as he dived in.

He knew what he would find and he had found it. At the fallen traffic pylon on the corner of the street – the one farthest away from the body – Technical Inspector Matthews, glancing around, put his hand over a tiny glob of silver material on the road and wondered if anyone had seen. No one had. He was kneeling down with his back to the people in the street and, to their minds, he was in his own little world doing what only he understood.

Under the palm of his hand he felt the little silver globule roll first one way and then the other.

It was part of a mercury tilt switch, part of an electrical bomb circuit so perfect in its simplicity that all it would have taken to set it off under normal circumstances would have been a truck passing by or, under abnormal circumstances, the blast of a gunshot fired anywhere in the general area and not – not at all – even directly at the bomb.

He knew exactly how much mercury the switch needed. He knew, precisely, how it was made.

It was the way, in all the counter-terrorist lectures he had given all over Asia in the last ten years, he had made them himself.

A little down the street there was what was left of a man.

In Sepoy Street, all the bodies had been burned black.

Still kneeling to hide what he had found, Matthews, his hand covering the little ball of rolling fluid metal, for the moment, decided to keep the information to himself.

It was 5.48 a.m. and behind him, in the street, he heard only silence.

In the Detectives' Room, O'Yee, patting the dog, said, smiling, 'Yeah, I slept well. How about you?' He had woken up in one of the cells with the dog asleep at his feet. He felt good, happy. At his desk the phone rang and, wrenching it up expectantly, for one wonderful moment he thought it might have been Emily and the children ringing from America.

He had been a field supervisor for the Department Of Main Roads. He had been the one who had told them exactly where to place the bombs. In the tile-lined post mortem room of the Mortuary, Feiffer, smoking a cigarette against the smell, waited while the Government Medical Officer cut away the remnants of Collins' coat and shirt and, giving the rags a quick flick to shake them, handed them over. He was also smoking: pungent, unfiltered French Gauloises. On the steel tray below the rising blue smoke from his cigarette there was not a clothed man: there was merely a series of parcels of meat wrapped in material. On what was left of Collins' left arm the cuff and part of his shirt was embedded deeply in a wound. Macarthur, snipping carefully with his long silver scissors, cut it away. It was merely a scrap of caked bloody linen. He reached down and put it on the steel table where the legs were. Macarthur, glancing at Feiffer turning the remnants of the clothes one way and then the other looking for pockets, said through his miasma of smoke, 'What exactly are you looking for?'

The pockets were all thick with dried blood. It was like putting your hand into a wound. Feiffer, extracting a silver Ronson lighter from a coat pocket and glancing at it for a moment, ran his hand hard down the seams of the material.

'Who was he?'

There was nothing in the seams. Feiffer, turning the coat around and reaching into the top handkerchief pocket to find only a collection of out of date used tram and bus tickets, said evenly, 'He was a man who wanted to go home.' On the tray Collins' head was turned away towards the steel door that led to Pathology. He seemed to be staring at it. All around there were more closed doors: they led to the cold rooms where the bodies from Sepoy Street waited in drawers for their turn to be examined on the steel table. The smell was awful. It was not coming from Collins. It was coming from the room itself. It was the ante room to extinction. Feiffer, putting out his cigarette on the floor and crushing it, took the remnants of the sleeve from near the legs and looked at it. By it, Macarthur, having reduced the dressed torso to naked white bloody meat, took up part of the hip and began cutting away at the shredded leather belt that held Collins' trousers to it. Only half the pelvic area was there. Part of the left hip had been completely blown away in the blast and it had not been found. Macarthur, snipping at the fob pocket, cut a wide oval section and, flipping it over with the point of his scissors to display it, said with a shake of his head, 'Nothing. He doesn't seem to have been carrying much on his person at all.'

There was not going to be anything. Feiffer, sliding his hand down with distaste into the hip pocket of the bloody, sliced trousers and finding nothing, said softly, 'No.' He wanted very badly to get out but there was nowhere to go. There was not even a clock in the room. Feiffer, putting his hand into part of another pocket on the trousers – what was left of the other hip pocket – finding nothing, ran his fingers down the seams and, also . . . found nothing. He heard Macarthur say with interest, 'Harry –' and looking up Feiffer asked quickly, 'What?'

'You don't have to stay for the post mortem. I can send you the results.'

He did have to stay. If there was nothing found, the one thing he would have to do was stay. Feiffer, watching Macarthur's scissors as they kept snipping, said with a trace of desperation in his voice, 'Anything?' Macarthur for all his tall, chain-smoking, cadaverous appearance, had soft, sad eyes. Feiffer said quietly, 'I need something, Tony. I need anything –'

Macarthur, snipping, said, 'What's this?' He had something in his hand: a bloody, caked piece of absorbent paper. It had come from Collins' trousers pocket. Macarthur, reading the legend printed on it, said, '*Alice's Bar, Wanchai Street, Hong Bay* – does that mean anything to you?'

It was all no good, hopeless. It was all no good and hopeless and whatever he did it was all too late or it was wrong. Feiffer said softly, 'Yes, it means something to me.' For a moment, he raised his hand to touch his eyes, but his hand was thick with blood. Feiffer, on the verge of surrender, said softly, 'Yes.' There was something else on the little drink coaster, written on the back, and, in the bright overhead light above the tray he tried to read it. It was probably nothing more than a drinks order. Feiffer, turning the paper first one way and then the other, asked, 'Can you read that?' Whatever it was had been written with the faint lines of a propelling pencil. The blood and fluids had almost obliterated it.

Macarthur, not looking at it, but at Feiffer, said with concern, 'Look, this is my department. The people who come in here are all strangers to me. I can send you the report just as easily –'

'Can you read what it says!'

'Yes!' Macarthur, taking the coaster and holding it up to the light in exactly the right position to make out the words and marks, said easily, 'It's a little map of a street.' He twisted the coaster a fraction. 'It's a little map of a street with the name of a man written underneath it with an exclamation point and –' he said curiously, 'and a huge dollar sign with more exclamation points after it. It says –' Macarthur waving his own cigarette smoke away said easily, 'It says *Sir Hercules Moore, 1838– 1907.*' He glanced at Feiffer, 'The drawing looks like a little representation of Moore's Pocket near Khartoum Street.' Macarthur, the smoke curling up around his head, said, 'Is that one of the streets they hit?'

No, it wasn't. *Alice's Bar, Wanchai Street, Hong Bay.* He had telephoned him from there at the Station. He had wanted to talk, but neither Feiffer nor he, at the time, had known what it was he had wanted to say.

Sir Hercules Moore, 1838–1907. Moore's Pocket, Hong Bay. No, it wasn't one of the streets they had hit.

At least, not yet.

Feiffer, freed, taking the coaster, not having to stay, said as the phone rang on the desk by Macarthur's hand and he went to answer it, 'No, it bloody well isn't.' The coaster was in his hand. It was *something*. It was the first thing. The call was for him. Taking the receiver from Macarthur's outstretched hand with the coaster gripped firmly in his fist, Feiffer, with heartfelt gratitude, said to the chain-smoking, cadaverous, nerveless man, 'Thank you. Thank you very much indeed!'

'Mr Collins, this is Detective Chief Inspector Feiffer. Earlier today when we spoke on the phone, I was in the middle of another matter and I – I just wondered if there was – If there was something you felt we should talk further about. I'm sorry

to have rung so late, but if there's anything you'd like to contact me about feel free to give me a ring tomorrow at the Station . . . Thank you.'

On the phone in the Detectives' Room, O'Yee reading back the transcript exactly, asked, 'Harry, did you make that call?'

'Yes.' On the line from the Mortuary, Feiffer's voice sounded strained. 'He called me earlier in the day and I – why, Christopher?'

'Was he married – Collins?'

'I don't think so. Why?' There was something in O'Yee's voice he did not like. Feiffer said, 'Why? What's happened?'

'I've just had Bill Spencer on the line. He and Phil Auden broke into Collins' apartment and they found a woman. Judging by a photograph and clothes they found they think she was probably his wife.' O'Yee said, 'A Chinese girl.'

'So?'

'So when Auden and Spencer went in the answering machine was still on and your message had wound itself back and it was still playing.' O'Yee said, 'It had one of those whistle attachments that means you can call up the message from a phone box. You didn't find the whistle on Collins' body, did you, by any chance?'

'No.'

'Then someone else must have called it up.' O'Yee said evenly, 'Bill Spencer says he has one of them on his own phone and when you call it up, a light goes on to register it. The light on Collins' phone was on. The woman must have seen it and run back the tape to hear what it said.' O'Yee said quickly before Feiffer could ask, 'She's dead, Harry. Someone almost decapitated her with a single shotgun blast at about four this morning when she came home from work. The neighbours heard it, but they were too frightened to investigate.' O'Yee, lowering his voice, said softly, 'Harry, it's only a guess, but according to Auden and Spencer, judging by the appearance of the body – by its placement in the room – she was listening to your message when she got killed.'

123

In the Mortuary there was no clock. There was no need. It was the ante room to extinction.

O'Yee, sounding worried, said urgently, 'Harry, you didn't know or suspect *yesterday* that Collins was one of the bombers, did you?'

It was 6.29 a.m.

It was the second day.

On the line from the Detectives' Room, hearing only silence, O'Yee said anxiously, 'Harry? Hullo? Harry – Harry, *are you still there?*'

11

At his bench, Technical Inspector Matthews took up a small glass tube fitted at each end with an electrical contact and pivoted, off-centre, on a little plastic balance fulcrum. The tube was empty. It was a demonstration mock-up of a mercury tilt switch.

All it needed, when fitted to a car or any installation where there might be movement or vibration, was a tiny globule of mercury to make an electrical connection at both ends when it moved.

It was a Police demonstration switch for a bomb.

He had the tiny globule of mercury from Khartoum Street in the palm of his hand, rolling backwards and forwards across his lifeline.

Opening one end of the glass tube, he cupped his hand.

The Police demonstration switch took, exactly, one half of one c.c. of mercury.

He let the mercury from his hand flow into the glass tube.

It was one half of one c.c. of mercury.

. . . exactly.

'The scenery, ever changing, never wearies the eye; but a great feature lies in the immediate surroundings; the trees, ferns, flowers, birds and butterflies. Along the length of Khartoum Street the visitor will probably see more of this life flitting in

and out than anywhere else. The path is perfectly level and the eye is so frequently diverted from one object to another that twilight approaches all too soon. The quaintly named Moore's Pocket, so-called in memorial to the late Sir Hercules Moore of recent tragedy, forms a little watering-hole, an oasis where, away from the raucous cries of the rickshaw and sedan chair bearers one may enjoy the bracing sea breezes and briefly restore oneself for the continuance of the tour: an easy thirty minute walk to North Point and the fragrant and blossom-filled gardens of Hanford Hill . . .'

On the wall phone in the corridor of the Singapore Road apartments, Feiffer, gripping hard at the instrument, said tightly to the Commander on the other end of the line, 'No, Neal, I don't know what it means. All I know is that I found it in Collins' apartment and the section I quoted to you was marked in pencil.' All he had was that and a beer coaster from a bar in Wanchai Street. 'It's from a 1911 brochure put out by Thomas Cook's called *Information For Travellers Landing In Hong Kong* and I assume Collins picked it up somewhere in a street market and marked the page.' It was nothing. It was only, for the second time, the name of a man a street had been called after.

Through the open door of the apartment he could see the girl. By the body Spencer was bending down searching for shell cases. He put his hand down on the floor to steady himself for a moment and when he straightened up his hand came away covered in blood. Feiffer, glancing away, said tightly, 'All I know is that Collins, I think, wanted to tell me something, but whatever it was it didn't stop him going out with his pals to destroy another street the moment he was sober and, whatever it was, it got him killed!' In the room, there was the sound of talk. Scientific were in the apartment. They were trying to decide on Auden's instructions just which wall panel to start ripping out first. Feiffer said, 'O.K.? Is that a fair summary? When he spoke to me from the bar I got a very niggling sort of feeling and, much too late for anyone – for Collins, for the girl

– for anyone at all – I left him a message on his bloody little machine and when the poor bloody bitch in here got her fucking head blown off it was still playing!' He was holding on with an effort, but it was no good. In the room, Spencer was looking at his hand and glancing around for something to wipe it on. There was nothing. All there was was blood. Feiffer, crushing the little brochure in his hand and trying to push himself closer to the wall to get into it, through it, past it – anywhere, *away* – said shaking, '*All right?* Is that about the size of it? Is that the way it bloody was?'

'It could be just a curio he picked up years ago. For all you know, the pencil mark on the page –'

'He wrote it on the beer coaster: Sir Hercules Moore, 1838 to 1907. With a bloody dollar sign. And a map of Moore's Pocket!'

'Take it easy.' The Commander's voice was soothing, calm. 'What about the girl?'

'What about her?'

'Who was she? His wife?'

'No. According to the neighbours, she moved in with him a few years ago, but she wasn't –' Feiffer said quickly, 'Look, there was a history of Hong Kong on Collins' bookshelf and I looked up this man Moore and he was an English financier who ran something called the Philippines Opium Trading Bank in what was then called Birdcage Street until the opium trade with the Philippines was suddenly stopped in 1903 and he was ruined.' From the room, he could hear the sounds of ripping and tearing as a panel came down. 'He was over extended on payments to middle men in Manila and Luzon and after an unsuccessful attempt to reorganize his finances, he put a bullet into himself.' In the apartment they had used a shotgun at close range. Feiffer, seeing Spencer looking at him with the blood still on his hand, said urgently, 'It's Moore's Pocket. Whatever they're planning to do it's going to take place in Moore's Pocket.'

'Based on the fact of a 1911 tourist guide and a bloody beer coaster?'

'Based on the fact that he wanted to talk to me! Based on the fact that so far they've killed God knows how many people by bloody accident and at least two by design and based on the fact that, whatever they're going to do, has to be done fairly quickly – based on the fact that two unaccidental killings mean that it's starting to go wrong.'

At the body, the stretcher bearers from the Morgue had their hands under the dead girl's shoulders. She had been twenty-eight or twenty-nine years old. Like Collins, she would end up on a steel tray being turned into nothing more than a carcase. Feiffer, glancing away, said with an effort at reasonableness, 'There's nothing I can do here. Auden and Spencer are both capable of following up the girl. I think what I should do is –' He tried to look away, but it was no good. Everywhere there seemed to be nothing but death. Feiffer, wiping at his face, losing his thread, said, feeling lost, 'Look –'

'Harry, there's nothing in Moore's Pocket. All there is are a few commercial buildings of very little importance, a couple of offices and the odd –'

'I know that.'

'I've checked and there aren't any high value loads either in or passing through Moore's Pocket. There's nothing. All Moore's Pocket is is a little feeder road on the way to the flyover –'

'I know that, Neal.'

'Harry, they're not trying to stop the traffic. According to Chief Inspector Kyle-Foxby, who's something of an acknowledged expert on this sort of thing, the only effect they've had is to speed the traffic up. Now if Moore's Pocket, which is only about a hundred and fifty feet long, is somehow supposed to be a stopping place then I'm buggered if I can see how –'

'*It's all I've bloody got.*'

'The girl –'

'The girl was listening to the message I left when she got killed!'

'Maybe she knew something. Maybe if Collins was going to tell you something he also –'

'If he told her anything –' In the apartment, they were lifting the body. For an instant, Feiffer saw the wound the gun had made. 'If he told her anything – He told me he didn't have anyone at home to go to. If he was going to tell her anything why was he in a bar ringing up cops he hardly knew and drivelling about bloody Scotland and –' It was too much. There was just too much death and blood and ruined flesh. He saw Spencer looking down at his bloody hand. 'He didn't tell her anything. He told *me* something. He couldn't bring himself to talk on the phone so he –' Cook's little brown 1911 guide book was nothing. It could have been marked by anyone. Feiffer, on the edge of desperation, said without room for discussion, 'It's Moore's Pocket! Whatever's going to happen is going to happen in Moore's Pocket!'

'I suppose you can ask that man Nonte about it –'

'I don't have to ask bloody Nonte! You're right. There's nothing in Moore's Pocket! O.K.? All right? *But I don't have anything else to go on!*'

'You've got the girl.'

'Auden and Spencer can do the girl.'

There was a silence. In that silence, they began carrying what was left of the girl out into the corridor.

In the silence, Feiffer, looking away, said quietly, 'Neal, they've killed over fourteen people on the streets in two days. I have to go with the numbers.'

'All right, Harry.' From the Commander's end of the line there was a pause.

'They can't keep it up, Neal. It has to be today. Whatever they're planning, it has to happen today.'

'Technical Inspector Matthews, according to his report, doesn't think they're planning anything . . .'

'It isn't a bloody *game*! They're doing something for a purpose!' He was shouting. Feiffer, his fist pressed hard against the wall, gritting his eyes closed as the body went by, said with vehement conviction, 'I don't know what it is and I don't know why they're speeding up the traffic – and I don't even know if that's what they're doing – but I swear to God I know they're doing something.'

'But *what?*'

'*I don't know what!*' Everywhere there were the dead, everywhere. There was no respite from them. They were everywhere. He saw the single black Shensi work slipper. Feiffer, out of control, yelled as the body went by and in the room Scientific began smashing down the wall panels in earnest to search the place, 'All I know is that whatever they're doing they can't – *they can't keep it up!*'

'They can't, Harry? Or you can't?'

'They're doing something! I know they are and whatever it is, it's got something to do with Moore's Pocket.' For a moment, as the sheet on the stretcher moved, he saw the girl's face. Feiffer, trying to find somewhere else to look and finding nowhere, lowering his voice, said at the edge of desperation, 'For God's sake, Neal, Auden and Spencer can find out who she was, can't they?' He said softly, 'Please.'

It was Moore's Pocket. It was all he had.

From the open apartment door, Auden said softly, calling to attract his attention, 'Boss –?' He shook his head. They were not going to find anything in the apartment.

On the phone, Feiffer said softly, 'Neal, please . . .'

The girl had gone. The sounds of tearing had stopped from the apartment. There was nothing there.

On the phone, begging, Feiffer said again, 'Neal, please . . .'

'*Mr Collins, this is Detective Chief Inspector Feiffer. Earlier today when we spoke on the phone . . .*'

In the apartment, Scientific at the answering machine, were playing the message over and over.

It was 7.57 a.m. on the second day.

Feiffer, hiding, pressing himself in hard against the wall, afraid to look at anything more he might have to see, yelled desperately into the phone above the sound, 'Neal, for Christ's sake –'

'*Mr Collins, this is Detective Chief Inspector Feiffer. Earlier today . . .*'

'For Christ's sake, Neal —!'
'— when we spoke on the phone . . .'
'Mr Collins, this is Detective Chief Inspector Feiffer. Earlier today when we spoke . . .'
He had killed them both, Collins and the girl. As surely as if . . .
'Mr Collins, this is Detective Chief Inspector . . .'
At the phone Feiffer said in total awful supplication, 'Neal, for Christ's sake! Please. Don't you see? It's all I've got left.'

Isandula Street . . .
Sepoy Street . . .
General Gordon Street . . .
In the computer room in Traffic, Chief Inspector Kyle-Foxby, tapping up the schematics, said softly over and over, 'Bastard! Bastard!'
They were coming onto the screen, graphics of all the streets with representations of all the traffic flows that used them and their rate.
There were little symbols, marks, flashing lights, showing all the activity on all the streets.
He kept tapping away at the console for more information.
He thought of Feiffer.
In the drawer of his office on the next floor, there was his regulation issue Smith and Wesson Highway Patrolman .357 magnum revolver still in its regulation issue holster.
It was never loaded and he never took it home with him at night.
On the flickering screen, Kyle-Foxby, his gaze fixed, watched the representation of the traffic as, in its little pro-grammed circuits, it flowed never-endingly around in a giant circle in the worst run and worst planned system of roads in the world.
Kyle-Foxby thought of his little lectures to his men. He thought of Good Germs and Bad Germs.
He thought of Feiffer.

Kyle-Foxby said in a snarl, 'You dirty, lousy, stupid, stinking – *bastard!*'

His eyes stayed fixed on the screen.

His fingers, with practised ease, with a life of their own, kept tapping at the keyboard.

In Moore's Pocket the man of limited time, watching the traffic, wondered about the girl.

He wondered if what had been done upset him.

It didn't. It had simply been done.

8.27 a.m.

He was always on time, never wrong.

The traffic fascinated him.

There was only a limited amount of time to go – required.

Standing in the street, watching the traffic, with his fingers drumming against the side of the leg, he wondered if he had made a mistake about the girl . . .

'Mrs Collins worked the switchboard here from eight at night until three in the morning four days a week.' At reception in the Goddess Of The Sea Hotel on Fisherman's Road, the Proprietor, a short, fat sweating man named Two Minute Tan, said firmly, 'I don't want any trouble.' It wasn't a hotel at all, it was a series of streetwalkers' doorways with beds. Two Minute Tan, glancing up the paint-flaking wooden stairs that led to the source of his income, put his hand in his pocket and, glancing at the unlit switchboard, said, 'No trouble: that's what I live for. I spend my entire life making sure I sleep nights.'

It was more than anyone else did in the place. Spencer, running his eyes across the carpeted floor of what was little more than an alcove in an alcove, said, nodding, 'Fine.' He asked, 'Mrs Collins, did she –'

'She worked the switchboard.'

'Did she ever go by any other name?'

'No.' Two Minute Tan looked at Auden. Auden was a big one. He wasn't saying anything. Auden had his gaze fixed firmly on Tan's hand in his pocket and there was the faintest smile playing about his face. Two Minute Tan said firmly, 'She was married to a man in the Main Roads Department.'

'No, she wasn't.'

Two Minute Tan said, 'Oh?' He looked up the stairs again. Up there, from all the rooms, there was silence. He had pressed a button somewhere under his desk and anyone who was up there doing whatever they were doing at half past nine in the morning was going to stay up there doing it or, if they had already done it, pretend they had done nothing until the cops had gone. Two Minute Tan, taking his hand out of his pocket and patting it, said with a smile, 'Should I be shocked at her immorality?'

Auden was still faintly smiling, still watching the hand on the pocket. Auden said tonelessly, 'She's dead. Someone killed her.'

'Well, it wasn't me.'

Spencer said, 'What was her real name?'

Auden asked, 'Was she a whore?'

'No, she was a respectable woman married to a European.' Two Minute Tan said, 'Protection. It doesn't hurt.' He put his hand back in his pocket and grinned. 'No trouble, that's my motto. I'll do anything to avoid trouble.'

Spencer asked again, 'What was her real name?'

'I don't know.' Two Minute Tan, relaxing, said pleasantly, 'Maybe she was an illegal. Maybe she was a poor refugee from the evils of Communist China I was kind enough to employ with no questions asked. Maybe all it says on her identity card is —'

'All it says on her identity card is Mrs Collins.'

'Then she was an illegal. Then all you have to do is go to the Illegals Register and —'

Auden, still smiling, said calmly, 'Gee, what a good idea.' He looked at Spencer. 'Why didn't we think of that?' His eyes moved to Two Minute Tan's pocket. 'The only trouble is that we need her original name to look her up. Isn't that a pity?' Auden said quietly, 'You see, the problem is that we've just

133

spent a long while looking at what was left of a human being after someone hit her with a shotgun and if you think what we'd really like to do now is stand here and listen to you play games and pretend you're going to offer us a bribe to go away, then you're wrong.' He was still smiling. He turned to Spencer. 'Isn't that right, Bill?' Still smiling, he asked Spencer, 'See how calm I am? It's learning that I can make my way in the world without violence that does it.' Reaching over and taking Two Minute Tan by the scruff of the neck and hauling him up onto the desk, Auden asked, still smiling, 'What was her real name please? So far life has taken on a new meaning of non-violence to me and I'd hate it if you went and spoiled it now.' He had Two Minute Tan's neck caught in the scruff. He twisted it. Auden, suddenly going cold, shouted, 'We've just had to look at a poor girl with her goddamned head blown off and you've got exactly two and a half seconds to answer before you go the same fucking way.'

Two Minute Tan, going red, yelled, 'Lee! Her real name was Lee. She was an illegal.' He still had his hand in his pocket. Two Minute Tan, his eyes bulging, yelled, 'I don't want any trouble. Her name was Lee. She was good for me – She was married to a cop. Before she – before she went to live with Collins, she told me she was married to a cop. In the Bomb Squad. A European. She liked Europeans, she –' Auden's grip was getting tighter. Two Minute Tan yelled, 'What the hell's wrong with you? Why can't you be reasonable? I'm prepared to pay to keep out of trouble – what's wrong with that? That's reasonable, isn't it?'

Auden said, 'Sure.' He looked up the stairs. There was no one about.

Spencer said quietly, 'Let him go, Phil.'

Auden said, 'Sure.' He let him go.

Two Minute Tan, rubbing at his neck, pouting, said softly, 'You stupid bloody ignoramus.' Only a millisecond before Auden, reaching over the desk, drew back his fist and with a punch that sent him sprawling against the switchboard and lit it all up, at last, finally, righteously, got him to take his hand out of his lousy, goddamned, stinking, bribe money for the dead coat pocket.

He didn't live in the apartment on Singapore Road, he lived here. In Collins' office in the Department Of Main Roads building on Wyang Street, Feiffer, opening drawers and cupboards and finding bottles, asked, 'Did he sleep here too?'

'Sometimes.' Collins' Number Two in the Field Supervisors' Section was a short, plain, dumpy Chinese girl wearing slacks and a blouse. Watching from the door, she nodded. She looked at the empty and half full bottles that had been hidden all over the room. 'He was a drunk.' The girl, looking down at the close clipped nails on her fingers said softly, 'I'm better educated than he was, better qualified, better at the job, but he was Number One here because he was a particular sort of drunk for an engineer – he was a Scottish drunk.'

Standing there watching, she made a sniffing sound. 'The Scots invented the profession of engineering – at least according to the Empire and the Empire that gave you feet, yards, miles, acres, roods and perches, also gave as one of its lasting gifts the impression that unless you were Scottish you weren't qualified to touch anything that even vaguely resembled a road or a machine or a ship's boiler.' She sounded very bitter. The girl, glancing again at her nails, said softly, 'It's reassuring to have a few Och Ayes thrown in when your sewage pipes back up. It's like a cool British voice at the controls of a falling airliner: it calms the passengers down and makes them think the pilot knows something they don't. The Chinese built a few small things themselves like the Great Wall and the longest canals in the history of the world, but when it comes to promotion around here what counted was who invented a new surface for roads a hundred years ago – and that was a Scotsman named Macadam.' She asked, 'Is there anything in particular you're looking for?'

'I'm looking for the plans of Moore's Pocket.'

'You won't find them.' Everything in the room was a mess. The girl, sighing, said without rancour, 'He loaned things out.

I tried to keep track in the vain hope that when he finally drank himself to death or got back to Scotland I might take over, but – I've got a register of where everything went, but lately – in the last few weeks – when the drinking got really bad, I was afraid to come in here so the register is incomplete.' She saw Feiffer searching through the pigeon holes marked *Street Charts* and asked, 'Anything?'

'Nothing.'

'Then I'll get my register.' Her nails were clipped and she had given up everything to be what she had wanted to be. Whatever it was, unless the Chinese took over tomorrow and, by coincidence, she happened to be a trustworthy Communist, she was never going to achieve it. The girl said, 'I think he loaned them out to a friend of his – another European – but I'll check.' There was a slip of paper in one of the pigeon holes: the one marked *Sepoy Street* and Feiffer, taking it out, held it up for her to see. The slip was marked only with three initials: A.J.N.

The girl, pausing for a second to nod knowingly at the slip, said with deep bitterness, 'Sure. Him. His mate. Another European. A.J.N. He's got the Moore's Pocket map too.' She said with a bitter twist to her face, 'Albert John Nonte. He's the local toponomist.' She asked quietly, 'Do you know what that is?'

She seemed on the edge of tears.

It was Nonte. Looking at the slips in all the empty pigeon holes for Isandula Street, Sepoy Street, General Gordon Street, Khartoum Street, it was all Nonte.

A.J.N. Albert John Nonte.

He had had the plans for Moore's Pocket out now for over nine weeks.

It was 9.48 a.m. on what he was sure was the last day.

'Mr Collins, this is Detective Chief Inspector Feiffer . . .'

It was Moore's Pocket.

It was Nonte.

In the empty, bottle-strewn office on Wyang Street as the girl watched him as she watched all Europeans, with hatred

136

in her heart, Feiffer said quietly, 'Yes, I know what that is.'

It was Nonte.

The girl, standing at the open door, was watching.

She looked at the empty bottles in the room and shook her head.

In Collins' office, the phone rang. It was Bill Spencer ringing from a hotel on Fisherman's Road. He wanted to know whether Technical Inspector Matthews of the Bomb Squad had ever been married and, if he had, whether his wife had been a Chinese girl.

There had been at least five of them in the street when the bombs had gone off and taken out Kyle-Foxby's Land Rover, four of them on the corners of the streets and one at his car with the shotgun.

One of them had used that shotgun on the girl.

There were no other Europeans in the Bomb Squad.

Nonte, Collins – there had been five of them.

9.53 a.m.

Feiffer, gripping the phone hard as, from the open door, the Chinese girl went on watching him, said with sudden anger, 'I don't know. I'm not sure. What the hell are you asking me for? *Find out!*'

9.53 a.m.

It was the last day. He knew it.

Isandula Street, General Gordon Street, Sepoy Street, Khartoum Street, all of it – he wondered, suddenly lost, just what, in God's name, it was supposed to *achieve*.

12

'Oh, dear, oh, dear . . .' On the phone from the U.S. Embassy, Errol Cantrell, stifling a laugh, said happily, 'Oh, dear, oh, dear, Christopher, an official enquiry? Oh, dear, oh, dear. If I don't give the information you want what are you going to do: hit me with about seven hundred parking tickets?' He was making chuckling noises. 'You seem to forget I've got diplomatic immunity and I collect parking tickets as wall paper – as well as which, these days, having progressed to the dizzy heights of Third Secretary in the service of Uncle Sam and the American Way Of Life my driver is the one who gets all the parking tickets.' There was a pause from O'Yee's end of the line and Cantrell said happily, 'Hullo, are you still there?'

'Can I talk to someone in the C.I.A., please?'

'Can you *what*?' The chuckling stopped. Cantrell, drawing a breath, said warningly, 'This is the United States Embassy in Hong Kong, the Cultural Attache's Office, and unless C.I.A., in this case, happens to stand for the *Chesapeake Illiterati Association*, I have no idea at all what you're talking about.' Cantrell said with an edge to his voice, 'What the hell do you think you're doing, Christopher? You can't just ring up the goddamned Embassy, tell them you want a whole lot of confidential information about an ex-employee and expect them to spill it all out to you over the phone!' Maybe it was for the benefit of the tape recorders attached to the phone and running in the basement of the building. 'There are channels! If you want information about Doctor Albert John Nonte, late of this Service, then I suggest you go about it the right way and –'

O'Yee had his hand on the dog's neck. Caressing dogs was supposed to be good therapy. So far, it wasn't working. O'Yee, a moment before Cantrell could start in on more of his 'Oh dears', said again, 'Errol, put me onto someone in the C.I.A.'

'There isn't anyone from the C.I.A. Don't you read the papers?' He was getting annoyed. 'Look, I happen to have known Nonte briefly – on a personal level – and I can tell you that if you're looking for something spooky about him there isn't anything. He was a career language expert with about four hundred and eight degrees in Chinese language and civilization and if he hadn't left, by now he probably would have been Ambassador to Peking and I would have been sweeping the carpets for him and saying, "Yes, Mr Ambassador, no, Mr Ambassador, three bags full, Mr Ambassador" – O.K.?' Cantrell, becoming even more annoyed, said with ice in his voice, 'Christopher, you're trading on my friendship.'

'Why did he leave?'

'He left to work for the Hong Kong government as a –'

'– as a toponomist.'

'Right.'

'A namer of streets.'

'If that's what it means, yes.'

'That's what it means.' The dog was at O'Yee's side. O'Yee pulled at its ears. He was going to need all the friends he could find. 'That's a hell of a step-down, isn't it?'

'Is it?'

'Isn't it?'

'Yes. Yes, all right. Yes, it's a hell of a stepdown.' Cantrell said tightly, 'Gee whiz, how about that? What do you want me to say? *I still work here.*'

'It's important, Errol.'

'Why?'

'I can't tell you that.'

'Then I can't tell you anything either.' Cantrell, trying to control himself, said tightly, 'Look, Christopher, I know you and Emily were good to me when I got posted to this god forsaken little pimple on the backside of China and I know that Emily and the kids are away and you're feeling a bit left out, and I'd be delighted, anytime you like, to repay your kindness by giving you an evening out, the pleasure of my company, or even the shirt off my back, but when it comes to handing out information about ex-Government employees and why they might have been kicked out of the Diplomatic Service –'

'Was he kicked out of the Diplomatic Service?'

'Yes, he was fucking kicked out of the Diplomatic Service!' Cantrell, irked, said suddenly, 'Now you've got me swearing. I'm like Nonte: I want to stay in Asia. There are some things you don't do if you want to stay in Asia and swearing is one of them. Oh, dear, oh dear . . .' Cantrell said, 'You goddamned motherfucker, what are you trying to do to me?'

'I'm trying to find out something about Albert John Nonte! I'm trying to find out anything about him! I'm trying to find out –'

'Why?'

'Because – because –' O'Yee said, 'Put me on to someone in the C.I.A.!'

'You never give up, do you?' Cantrell, his voice changed: the voice O'Yee knew from nights of drinking together, said suddenly, 'All right, Albert John Nonte – a brilliant career in the U.S. Foreign Service blighted: what do you want to know and why do you want to know it?'

O'Yee said evenly, 'He's killing people, Errol. We think he's one of the people behind the bombing in Sepoy Street where fourteen people were killed.' He waited.

There was a silence. Cantrell said evenly, 'He was a homosexual. He figured in a scandal in the Colony and it was felt – in high places – that he had the' – he thought for a moment – 'the propensity to embarrass us if he was ever posted to a sensitive –' He stopped again. 'He was the most brilliant bastard I've ever met in my life, but the sad fact of the matter was that he was openly, visibly, and totally imprudently gay, queer, bent, sissy and bloody homosexual!' Cantrell, sighing, said, 'What a waste.' He paused again, 'He was caught in the act with a member of the Hong Kong security forces here and after the security guy's wife got wind of it and divorced him there was no way it could be hushed up. So Nonte was asked to leave. Which he did – preferably the entire region – which he didn't. And he's now –' He seemed a little sad, 'naming streets.'

O'Yee said quickly, 'Who was the member of the local security forces?'

'I don't know.'

'You must know!'

'Well, I don't! It was years ago!' Cantrell, snarling again, said bitterly, 'I don't know every goddamned thing in the entire world.'

'Then put me on to someone in the C.I.A.'

'You *are* on to someone in the C.I.A.' Cantrell, also never going to get a posting to Peking, but for different reasons – for an organization he had joined in the glamour days straight out of college when he had not really known a thing about it – before the days of Agee and Latin America – said bitterly, 'All right. O.K. It was someone in the Hong Kong police Bomb Squad. All right? I don't know, I didn't investigate it. All I did was recommend we check Nonte out.' His voice was trembling. He said, 'I'll find out his name and get back to you – does that satisfy you?'

He asked quietly, 'O.K.? All right?' He said quietly, sadly, as in the Detectives' Room, feeling low, O'Yee patted the dog, 'You *are* on to someone in the C.I.A., as well you know. And look at the great, bloody wonderful jobs – the real glamour of international intrigue – he gets to do.'

'I'm sorry, Errol.' O'Yee, closing his eyes for a moment, said quietly, 'Look, I'm really –'

'Yeah.' There was a pause and then Cantrell said briskly, officially, 'Senior Detective Inspector O'Yee, this is the U.S. Embassy in Hong Kong – we'll get back to you directly.'

141

It was the second time that morning the Records Clerk in Police Personnel had been rung about the same man. This time there was no delay while he looked the answer up. The information he had given to Detective Inspector Spencer of Yellowthread Street was still clear in his mind and, this time, talking to a Senior Detective Inspector, moving up, he could give the impression of brisk efficiency.

The Records Clerk, answering O'Yee's question without pause, said in Cantonese, 'Technical Inspector Robert Matthews, aged 48, twenty three years eight months service, particular field of expertise explosives, present posting Bomb Squad, no, sir, according to our records, he is not and never has been married.'

He dealt in facts. He had no interest at all in speculation.

The Records Clerk, always pleased to make points where he could, asked helpfully, 'All right, sir? Does that answer your question fully?'

Lee Mah Lei . . . Mary Lee.

In the Illegals Office, there were no fewer than eighteen hundred illegally entered Mary Lees set out on typed dockets all awaiting coding for the computer. The theory was that if an illegal made a home run across the border to Hong Kong and found a protector, he or she then became a legal and went into the computer with whatever name they chose to use.

Mary Lee. It might as well have been Joan Smith.

There were at least eighteen hundred illegally entered Mary Lees waiting to go into the computer.

It could have been worse.

There were over eight thousand Vietnamese also waiting, also on little typed dockets.

Sitting at the information card strewn table in the ground floor sorting office of the Illegals Register Office, Auden stifled a sigh. He glanced at Spencer.

Auden, lighting a cigarette, said softly, 'Well . . .' He glanced at the dockets stacked high for the Vietnamese.

At least they were still alive.

Putting his cigarette down in a little tin ashtray, he and Spencer, at 10.28 a.m., each took up the first of their cards.

10.29 a.m.

In Moore's Pocket, watching the traffic, the man of limited time counted the hours.

He lit a cigarette and found his hand was shaking in expectation.

It was the last day.

He was in the last hours.

He felt a tingle of excitement.

He touched at his hair and, in a strangely feminine gesture, flicked it back over his temple with his fingers.

It wasn't even a real street. Set at the end of Khartoum Street, Moore's Pocket was nothing more than a widening of a thoroughfare that, at one time, must have had trees and benches and quiet places to sit. Without the street sign set high up on the side of a building, most people would have simply assumed it was a bulge in Khartoum Street to give the traffic pause before it speeded up on its way across Yellowthread Street to the flyover and then to Central and the ferries and the tunnel to Kowloon. It was nothing. It was not a Chinese street, not even a Hong Kong variation of a Chinese street – with its anonymous, grey brick and stone low three storey buildings it was a nineteenth century European square. It had the dreary commercial buildings and tiny, unwashed clerks' windows – all it needed to complete the picture was pigeons and cobble-stones.

At a public telephone inside the door of the sub Post Office at the Yellowthread Street end of the street, Feiffer asked above the sound of the traffic, 'Did you ring them?'

At the other end of the phone O'Yee said, 'Yes, I rang them.'

'And?'

O'Yee sounded upset. O'Yee, seeming to draw a breath, said quickly, 'And what they told me was that Nonte was dismissed from the Foreign Service because he'd been caught banging some guy from the Bomb Squad. Evidently the feeling was that if he had been posted to Peking, sooner or later, the C.I.A. was going to find itself in the position of having to either withdraw him or knock him off before he found a little Chinese boy lover in the Politburo and started spilling him everything he knew.' O'Yee said, 'I spoke to Errol Cantrell at the Embassy and he says he doesn't know the name of the Bomb Squad cop but he'll look it up.' He said quickly before Feiffer could ask, 'Yeah, I know: Two Minute Tan told Auden and Spencer that Collins' de facto had been married at one time to – someone in the Bomb Squad.' He said again before Feiffer could ask, 'No, I don't know if it's the same man and if it was Matthews then he kept the marriage a secret from everyone including the Police Records Office.'

'Where are Auden and Spencer now?'

'At the Illegals Office. They're looking for the name of the Collins' woman's original protector when she got permission to stay. Her maiden name – or at least the name she used when she entered the Colony – was Lee Mah Lei – Mary Lee. They're going through the records to locate the original application.' There was a pause and then O'Yee said warningly, 'You know there's no evidence against Nonte, Harry? That it's all just –'

'I know.' Gazing out into the road, Feiffer had the feeling he was being watched. He had had the feeling from the moment he had left the car in Khartoum Street and begun walking. Feiffer said, 'I understand that, Christopher.'

'Do you want some help, Harry?'

'No.'

'Where are you?' O'Yee sounded concerned.

'Moore's Pocket.' There was no one there, he was hidden from the street in the doorway of the sub post office, but he could not shake the feeling he was being watched.

'Harry, *what the hell are they doing?*'

'I don't know.' Feiffer, gazing out, watched the traffic. If anything, with all the streets cordoned off and closed, it was moving smoother, faster. Feiffer, gripping the phone, said, shaking his head, 'I don't know.' The feeling of someone's eyes on him made him nervous. There was no one watching. He felt someone. Feiffer, turning away from the street, asked, 'How's your dog?' He turned back to the street, but there was only the traffic.

'The dog's going to needle city in the morning.'

'Oh?' Feiffer said with genuine concern, 'I'm sorry to hear that. Why?'

'Why not?' That was what was bothering him. O'Yee, dropping his voice, not talking to Feiffer at all, said quietly, 'Why not? I've used him. He's been handy for me, but now, after I've used him all up, why not?'

'Cantrell?'

O'Yee said softly, 'Yeah.' There was a pause and then, O'Yee said abruptly, 'The moment I get the name of the Bomb Squad man involved with Nonte I'll get back to you. Where will you be?'

'I'll be here. I'll ring you.' Feiffer, gazing out at the traffic, with the invisible eyes still on him from somewhere, said with an effort at concentration, 'Christopher look, about the dog —' He glanced at his watch. 11 a.m. exactly. He couldn't shake the feeling that, from somewhere, someone was watching his every move, hearing his every word. Feiffer said, trying to think, 'Look, um, if you just —'

'No.'

'Look. *Listen*. Um —' The traffic was building up. As it approached the lunch time peak, with all the shutdown streets cordoned off and closed, it was going faster and faster. And someone was watching. There, in the street, there were eyes upon him. It was 11 a.m. exactly. Feiffer said, trying to think, 'Look, just give it —' He turned quickly, but in the street there was only the traffic. Feiffer said reasonably, 'Look, Christopher, you're not —' It was no good. It was no good at all. Feiffer, shaking his head, said desperately, 'Look, I'm sorry. I have to go.'

Everywhere there was the traffic and the eyes watching him. Putting down the phone, Feiffer went quickly down the two steps out into the street and gazed down the length of the road to see what was there.

There was only the traffic. Its sound, as it reached fortissimo, was deafening.

There was hardly a break in the flow anywhere and, standing there on the kerbside looking up and down Moore's Pocket for something that was not there, Feiffer, all the time, stronger and stronger, felt eyes watching his every move.

It was 11 a.m. exactly on the last day and he had to wait for a very long time for a break in the traffic to get across to the other side of the street.

It was there, looking at him. On the computer screen, somewhere amid the simulated grids of all the systems, flyovers and approach roads, it was there staring him in the face.

It was there: he knew it. They were doing something to the streets and whatever it was they had worked out, not on the Police Traffic computer, but in their heads and whatever it was they were doing, he could find it.

At the desk, touching buttons on the console, forming new grids on the screen and merging them with the old, Kyle-Foxby said softly to himself, 'Yes.'

It was his life. It was what he did. On the screen little white dots representing the calculated flow of traffic at any time of day or night chased each other up and down graphs representing the optimum usage of road surfaces vis-à-vis destination and speed correlations.

It had all been worked out by him. It was all neat, ordered, timed, set, planned and unchanging, like an hour-glass.

He tapped up Moore's Pocket into the central grid of the display. It was a representation of the morning rush hour: the traffic, merging from all over the district, passed quickly and easily along Khartoum Street, widened out briefly in Moore's Pocket before it passed over the intersection of Yellowthread Street, and then, liberated, flowed smoothly and at an allowable extra five miles an hour onto the flyover and then, without stopping or turning, directly onto the main motorways to —

The closing of Isandula Street and all the others had not hindered the flow of the traffic at all. What it had done was speed it up.

It was pointless. It was crazy.

Kyle-Foxby, leaning up closer to the screen and watching all the little moving, flashing lights, said softly to himself, 'It's mad. Why are they doing it?'

With all the side streets gone all they had done was turn the system into a gigantic race track where – for some insane reason known only to themselves – the traffic, going faster and faster, was actually getting where it wanted to quicker.

He touched at a button on a console that would speed up all the moving lights by a simulated extra five, ten, then fifteen miles an hour. He watched as the lights began moving faster and faster. He watched what was happening.

Ten miles an hour extra simulated speed. He touched the button.

He watched what happened on the screen.

Kyle-Foxby, his eyes wide with horror, said suddenly, 'Oh my God.'

He had it. He knew what they were doing. All it was going to take was one more bomb and then –

He touched a button and speeded up the traffic by another five miles an hour.

All the streets and roads around the flyover led through Moore's Pocket. It was the only way to go.

Using the console with difficulty as his hands trembled on the buttons, he began closing down the simulated streets around it on the screen one by one to see what would happen.

He knew what was going to happen.

The only question in his mind was where.

Leaning close to the screen, steadying his hands, Chief Inspector Kyle-Foxby, doing what he knew how to do best, steadied his hands and began working it all out logically, calmly, piece by piece, a little organized systematic part of the puzzle at a time.

*

He had never shown anyone in his counter-terrorist demonstrations how to make a bomb. No one. Ever. He had always taken the made-up demonstration bombs into the lectures with him and shown his audiences, instead, how to detect them and, on special occasions, to the Police and the Army, how to take them apart.

He had never taken a wire and twisted it to make a connection anywhere other than in his lab: he had never, never shown anyone how to make a tilt switch using just the right amount of mercury to close a circuit and set a detonator off.

In his basement lab, bent over his bench gazing at the wire and the mercury, Technical Inspector Matthews, as always, alone in the room, said softly to himself, 'No, I never did.'

He was an expert, an artist: he always worked professionally and, like all artists, without assistance.

He touched at the twist in the wire and knew that it was his twist – the way only he did it.

Everywhere in the room, on shelves, in schematic drawings, there were the devices and instruments of sudden explosive death. Matthews, gazing at them, trying to think, said aloud, 'No, I never did. I never showed anyone how to do it.' He was sure. He tried to think back. Touching at the wire with his fingertips, feeling the twist he always put in it, his signature, there was no one.

He picked up the wire and felt its shape on the palm of his hand and, for a brief instant, thought he remembered a face.

No, it wasn't a face. What he remembered was a presence: eyes. The presence of eyes watching him. It had been a very long time ago. He looked around. It had been in this room.

He was no good at names. What he knew about was bombs.

Rolling the twisted wire back and forth on the palm of his hand, he tried to think who, a very long time ago, welcomed, invited, interested, watching him make his mock-up bombs for demonstrations – who, *who* had once been in his room with him.

He saw a face.

He touched the wire to his hand, and, closing his eyes, tried to put a name to it.

11.08 a.m.

In his silent, lethal room, Matthews, rolling the twisted wire gently, tenderly against the palm of his hand, narrowed his eyes and, gazing at the display of grenades on the shelf across from him, slowly and carefully began to try to think it through.

There was nothing. There was nothing on the street except the old commercial buildings of Empire and the old, run-down trading and financial institutions that had paid for it. On the sides of some of the buildings, faint and fading, Feiffer could actually see the names of some of the long-dead companies that once, when silk and tea and opium had been the mainstay of an Empire, had brought sweating, anxious clerks to their little rooms from half a world away to make their fortunes.

. . . where, away from the raucous cries of the rickshaw and sedan chair bearers one may enjoy the bracing sea breezes and briefly restore oneself . . .

Not any more. It was all dead, gone: it was the last street in the last Colony on the face of the globe.

. . . for the continuance of the tour . . .

And someone was watching him.

It was dead, finished. Like Sir Hercules Moore, with a self-inflicted bullet in his head after the collapse of the Philippines Opium Trade in 1907, it was nothing: a memory, an echo – there was nothing worth having there at all. The moment people like Kyle-Foxby got permission it was all going to be torn down and turned into one gigantic highway that stretched from Hong Bay, probably to the Moon. It was crazy. *There was nothing there.*

And someone was watching. He felt it.

11.09 a.m.

In the street, deafened by the traffic, walking back and forth, looking for he knew not what, Feiffer, touching at his face, said softly, 'Damn it! God bloody damn it!'

He was standing a little down from the intersection with

Yellowthread Street outside the paint peeling two storey brick building that once had housed the South African Embassy and now, with both the decay of the street and, coincidentally, South Africa's reputation in the world, now housed only a three room Consulate. It was nothing. It was like everything else in Moore's Pocket: it was no longer of any value at all.

He was being watched. He felt it.

There was no one there.

A little down the road where once there had been the raucous cries of the rickshaw men and the sedan chair carriers there was the office of someone he knew and, much too early for it to do any good, Feiffer began walking slowly towards it to ring O'Yee again about the Bomb Squad man.

He was being watched. He felt it.

The street, apart from the traffic, was empty and there was no one there.

11.10 a.m.

In Moore's Pocket, walking, being watched, he was totally, completely . . . alone.

13

In the Station, O'Yee was still waiting for Cantrell to call back.

In the front office of the Hong Bay Alarm Company, Henry Yu, still wearing the grey dust jacket he had worn in Sepoy Street when he had stopped all the alarms, lighting Feiffer's cigarette for him with a Zippo lighter, said shaking his head, 'Sir Hercules Moore? I've heard of him vaguely – probably sometime at school, like all kids in this Colony I wasn't sure whether I was supposed to be British or Chinese, but as for what he did –' He glanced over to a bench in the untidy room where two of his employees, identical twins named Wing, were repairing alarms. 'In when? 1907? I'm afraid it's beyond me.' The twins, like him were southern Chinese in their late twenties. Henry Yu, scratching his head, said with a smile, 'The old Philippines Opium Trading Bank or whatever it was called was where the Hong Bay Chartered Securities Company is now at the end of the street, but as for any details about it –' He shrugged. 'Isn't there some sort of historian or someone you could ask?'

There was only Nonte. He had looked at the Hong Bay Chartered Securities Company. It was opposite the South African Consulate. It was a one roomed office behind a glass door. It was nothing. Feiffer, glancing at the twins at their bench repairing circuitry, asked, 'What about alarms, Henry?

Is there anything in this street with special security arrangements – any sort of elaborate alarm system you put in?' He saw Yu start to shake his head. 'Anything at all?'

'No. Nothing.' One of the twins, presumably speaking English, also shook his head. Yu said, 'No.' He thought for a moment. 'No. Nothing.' Summing up the state of the office, business was bad. Yu, following Feiffer's gaze, said sadly, 'The computer and the credit card has killed the high risk cash business. Even in Central District all we put in these days are fire alarms and the occasional small bell in jewellers' shops and places where there's a lot of valuable retail stock – but there isn't anything like that in Moore's Pocket.' He indicated his office. 'Moore's Pocket is a low rent district as you can see.' He pointed to the broken alarms on the table. 'They should be replaced with new systems but, these days, people just want the show of an alarm for insurance purposes. When the insurance companies realize that there's nothing worth protecting in their clients' premises other than a few computer print-outs – and that all you need to steal them is a code and a telephone – we'll be out on the streets with our begging bowls.' Yu said, 'I'm sorry, but if you think there's anything in Moore's Pocket then you've got the wrong street.'

'Yeah.' Feiffer glanced at the telephone.

'Do you want to ring your Station?' Yu, smiling, said pleasantly, 'The Hong Bay Alarm Company may be going out of business fast but we can still afford to give the forces of law and order the odd free phone call.'

'Thanks.'

'Well?'

'No.' Feiffer, glancing at his own watch, asked, 'What time is it?'

'Eleven twenty.' Yu, looking concerned, said thoughtfully, 'You look like something the cat dragged in. Why don't you –'

'Thanks anyway.' Glancing out through the open doors of the office, Feiffer could see the traffic. Outside, where the traffic was, there was Moore's Pocket. 'I'm sorry to hear business is bad. If I hear of anywhere that needs an alarm –'

'Yeah.' Yu, sighing, glancing at the Wing twins, said with a shrug, 'No, forget it. My two friends here have got an offer to go to work for a company in Macao making electronic toys and as for me —' He obviously didn't have anything. Yu said, 'Thanks anyway, but I think I'd better look for a new line of business.' He spoke faultless English. Feiffer wondered for a moment where he had learned it. 'I'm sorry you're barking up the wrong tree in Moore's Pocket, but I have to tell you as an expert there's absolutely nothing here of any value at all — except me.' Yu, grinning, said, 'And my value, with the onset of the plastic money revolution, is reducing day by day.' He turned to the twins at the table and said in Cantonese, 'It's all right for you people: you've got jobs to go to. What am I supposed to do?' He knew Feiffer spoke Cantonese. Yu, still grinning, asked in Cantonese, 'How about crime?' He saw Feiffer's face. It looked tired. Yu said quietly, 'Well, why not? But not in Moore's Pocket.' His voice was low, intimate. Yu said with concern, 'No, not here. Mr Feiffer, I tell you — honestly — there just isn't anything in Moore's Pocket worth having.' He asked again, 'Are you sure about the phone?'

Still gazing out at the traffic, Feiffer nodded. He had a sick feeling starting in his stomach.

11.22 a.m.

Henry Yu of the Hong Bay Alarm Company, full of his own troubles, said thoughtfully, 'If you're worried about the cost — you can always owe it to me.'

11.24 a.m. The moment he stepped out again into Moore's Pocket the eyes were upon him, watching.

The street, except for the traffic, was totally deserted.

The eyes watched every move he made. He could feel them.

There was no one else in the street.

The moment he stepped back onto the street he could feel the eyes. As if . . . as if they had been waiting for him.

There was absolutely no one else in the street at all.

He felt the eyes, secretly, move to follow him as he walked.

*

He saw him. He knew who he was. At his bench in the basement laboratory of the Scientific Branch on Aberdeen Street, Technical Inspector Matthews said suddenly, 'Yes! I remember you! Your idea of a good time was to put dud bloody booby traps under the seats of the bloody people I was lecturing to!' He remembered. He remembered a face, eyes watching him from behind the bench as, bit by bit, piece by piece, wire by wire, he had put fake bombs together to show the businessmen who, in the early days of the P.L.O. and international terrorism, had sat bored and complacent through his lectures and confided to each other over yawns that it was never going to happen to them.

He had shown them letter bombs, parcel explosives . . . mercury tilt switches.

It was never going to happen to them, and his assistant at the time — in the days when there had been money for anti-terrorism and the world was starting to wake up to a new sort of crime — his assistant at the time had gotten crapped off and started setting fake bombs under the audience's chairs to blast them out of their complacency.

He had watched every move as Matthews had built his little devices for him. *He had even built a few of them himself.* In his laboratory, Matthews, seeing his face again, said softly, 'Yes.'

Wires, mercury tilt switches — the hand of an artist. Matthews, gripping the twisted wire in his hand, said softly, 'Yes!' Matthews said in a gasp, 'My God, I saw him in Sepoy Street with that guy Collins from Main Roads!' He touched at the wire. 'My God, he was there checking up on his bloody work!' He said, 'Hmm —' He tried to think of the man's name. He had been his assistant for no more than six months eight or nine years ago and if he had ever called him anything, it would have been by his first name or his rank or —

He was a Sergeant. He had left the Bomb Squad when the first flush of terror had died down and people had gotten used to planes being hijacked and hands being blown off by letter bombs and he had gone on to —

No, he had left the Force. He had been caught in the middle

of a mucky divorce and he had – what? His name was Sergeant . . .

Sergeant . . .

Sergeant . . . what?

What?

Matthews, still holding the twisted wire in his hand, trying to think, reached for the phone to call Police Records to find out.

11.25 a.m.

He wondered why, for an instant, when he told the man his name, the Police Records Clerk seemed a little frightened.

LEE MAH LEI, b Kwantung province 7.6.57, illegal entry date . . .

In the Illegals Office, sifting his way through the mountain of cards, Spencer said suddenly, 'Got it.' He held up the card to Auden. 'Got her. I've got the right one.' He said in triumph, his eyes swimming with all the information he had digested, 'Look at it. It's her!'

LEE MAH LEI, b Kwantung province 7.6.57 . . . Spencer, reading off the information, said tightly, 'Reason For Permission To Stay; offer of marriage from local resident – occupation Police Officer.' Spencer, unable to believe his luck, said, 'Got her.'

Auden said, 'Matthews?'

'It doesn't say. All it says here is Police Officer – see card number 81693/A/0/231.' Spencer, rising, so close, said with a tremble in his voice, 'And that card isn't here strewn about on the table. That's a filing cabinet number and it's over there in one of those cabinets just waiting for us to dig it out.'

He couldn't believe his luck. He had found the card on only the ninth attempt. Spencer, going over to the cabinets and running his finger down the line of numbered labels, said quietly, '81693/A/0 . . .' He pulled out a drawer. '/0/231.' He found the card and said in a whisper, 'Here.'

Auden said without argument, 'It's Matthews, isn't it? She was married to Matthews in the Bomb Squad, wasn't she?' He

155

saw Spencer look at the card and then start to come over with it in his hand. Auden said, sure, 'Wasn't she? It's bloody Matthews, *isn't it?*'

It wasn't.

Auden , staring at the name on the card, said incredulously, '*Him?* Was he ever in the Bomb Squad?'

Spencer, nodding, his years in administration behind him but not forgotten, said, nodding, 'Yes, yes, he was. For about six months. I remember hearing about why he left.' He looked down at the name on the card and shook his head. 'He was queer. He got involved in a scandal with an American diplomat and the price of hushing it all up and keeping the diplomat's name out of the papers was his resignation.' Spencer, trying to recall the details, said, 'I don't know what happened to him after that but Police Records will.'

It was turning into a busy morning for the Police Records Clerk.

Still holding the card, so close to the answer, Spencer went quickly to find a phone to ring him.

There. He saw it. It was there on the Consulate, mounted high up on the second floor, half hidden by a carefully trimmed tree in the little front garden of the place, aimed exactly, professionally and all-encompassingly down and across the street.

It was opposite Sir Hercules Moore's old bank, opposite the Hong Bay Chartered Securities Company, opposite a one roomed glass doored office of no consequence on the corner of the street, watching.

Watching everything.

It was a ledge-mounted television monitor camera and, as Feiffer, on the other side of the road outside the Securities Company moved a little to see it, it moved to see him.

It was a single metal box mounted on a servo-driven swivel: a dark, polished eye, watching.

It was watching. It was watching everything.

In Moore's Pocket there was nothing to see.

11.28 a.m.

Outside the Hong Bay Chartered Securities Office, touching at the glass of the front doors that concealed, in the one room bank-like office, *nothing*, Feiffer watched as the camera, no longer moving, kept its unblinking eye directly on him.

The Consulate, outside, seemed deserted.

Moore's Pocket. In Moore's Pocket there was nothing to see except the traffic.

Below the camera, for an instant, he thought he saw the main door to the Consulate open a fraction and, touching at his gun to steady it in its holster as he ran, Feiffer went quickly through a break in the traffic across the street towards the door to catch it before it closed again.

The camera was still watching.

He saw it move.

They had closed off Isandula Street completely. It was out of the picture, finished. And General Gordon Street, with the meters gone, was nothing more than a speedway. Sepoy Street was gone, closed off. Khartoum Street and East Yellowthread Street, with the lights gone – uncontrollable: nothing more than a bottleneck for the traffic heading for the flyover. Moore's Pocket . . .

Moore's Pocket . . .

Good germ, bad germ . . .

Moore's Pocket . . .

All it was going to take was one more bomb and the ultimate nightmare would be there.

Kyle-Foxby, at his computer, touched at his face.

Moore's Pocket. The last bomb was going to be in Moore's Pocket. At his computer, punching it up, he watched as the traffic moved through its systems towards the flyover. It was going faster than it should, accelerating, speeding up, going through the bulge of the system towards the flyover faster and faster like water flowing suddenly from a leaking tank.

It was there: he knew it – the answer. All it was going to take was one more bomb. He had thought, in Sepoy Street and then

later, in Khartoum Street when they had tried to kill him, that
everything he had ever wanted was lost.

It wasn't lost. He was seconds away from the greatest
triumph of his life.

Good germ, bad germ.

At his console, tapping up the information, Kyle-Foxby, his
eyes bright and shining, said in a whisper, 'You bastards! I've
got you!' All it was going to take was one more bomb. All he
had to do on the computer was simulate it.

Touching at the buttons, destroying bits of the street a
single display line at a time, working carefully, slowly, logically, *systematically*, Kyle-Foxby said softly, 'You bastards,
I'm better than you are and that's why I'm going to beat you.'

He touched a button and tested a simulated bomb on the
traffic at the far end of the street where Moore's Pocket met
Khartoum Street.

He was so close. He knew he was going to win.

11.31 a.m.

With all the time in the world, Kyle-Foxby, single-mindedly,
went on ensuring that everything he had ever wanted in his life,
one day, rightfully, earned and worked-for, would be his.

On the phone Errol Cantrell said urgently, 'I've got it. It was in
the Confidential file and I had to use my special code to get it up
on screen, but now I've got it. It's the name of Nonte's
boyfriend in the Bomb Squad – the one who got him chucked
out and consigned to the lowly depths of toponomy.' He
sounded, for a moment, like the old Cantrell, full of enthusi-
asm and friendship. He wasn't. In the silence as O'Yee waited,
Cantrell, snapped, 'Hullo? Are you still there?'

'I'm still here.' At his desk, O'Yee had his hand on the dog's
head. O'Yee asked, 'This man in the Bomb Squad – was he
married?'

'Yeah, to a refugee named Mary Lee. That was another
reason Nonte had to go. Too mucky. She'd known him before
in China – the cop – before he came over to Hong Kong, and
the official feeling was that there was no way of checking that

the whole thing wasn't a set-up and the cop was Nonte's lover on a professional espionage basis. We did a deal and so did the cops: a nice quiet, uncontested divorce for the woman and a nice quiet resignation for Nonte and that way everyone was sure that—' He paused momentarily, '—that everyone had lost.' He asked, 'The Bomb Squad man — do you want his Chinese first name or his European one?'

'Both.' At his desk, O'Yee, not looking at it, patted the dog.

'O.K.' Cantrell, all efficiency, no longer a friend, said briskly, 'Right. Have you got a pencil? I'll give it to you slowly.'

It wasn't a Consulate at all. What it was was a two storey building with a coat of arms and a South African flag. And a camera.

At the half open door, Feiffer, pausing for a moment, touched at his gun. Above him, the camera was still. He felt eyes upon him, but they were no longer watching him through the camera — they were real.

He touched at the door and it opened. Inside, in the little tile floored hallway, there was nothing. The door moved easily. Somewhere, somewhere above him, set into the door jamb, he thought he saw, for an instant, a light blink. There was the faintest buzz: a metal detector.

It was not a Consulate at all. It was a dark, tile floored empty building. To his right, he thought he saw, just for a fraction of a second, something move behind a half open door. He heard a click.

11.36 a.m.

He knew the sound.

It was the sound of a gun being cocked.

In that room, out of sight, with a quick, jerking motion, as he came forward, someone cocked a gun.

On the phone to O'Yee, Auden said urgently, 'Christopher, we've got it. We've got the name. We know who the hell's

159

behind it.' He had the little card in his hand as Spencer, on the phone to Records, was saying, 'Where the hell is he now?' Auden said quickly, 'We know why the Collins' girl got herself knocked off. It was because she was married at one time to the bomber and whether or not Collins told her anything was beside the point. She knew who was involved because she was the one connection between them. After Collins was killed she had to go too.' He heard Spencer shouting at the Records Clerk to check his files. 'Where the hell's Harry?'

'He's in Moore's Pocket.' On the phone, O'Yee, trying to get it down on paper, said quickly, 'Nonte. It was probably Nonte. He was the Bomb Squad man's lover – he probably still is.' It was working, coming together. O'Yee said quickly, 'I've tried Nonte's number and there's no reply so whatever is going to happen is probably happening now.' There was no way to reach Feiffer. 'But no one knows what the hell it is they're going to do.' He heard the phone on Feiffer's desk ring and he went over carrying his own phone to answer it. He ordered Auden, 'Wait. Just wait. Wait a second.' He said urgently into the phone, 'Harry? Is that you?' It was Chief Inspector Kyle-Foxby from Traffic. O'Yee, too busy to talk, snarled, 'What the hell do you want?' He heard Auden say something in his other ear. He ordered him, 'Wait. Will you wait.' He heard Kyle-Foxby saying something about Moore's Pocket and he demanded, 'What the fuck are you talking about? What peak hour? The peak hours are at eight and five and at –' He looked at his watch. It was 11.37.

– and, in Moore's Pocket, exactly, always, because it was the opening of the bottleneck from Hong Bay into all the other districts for the lunchtime break traffic, exactly at noon.

11.37 a.m. It only took five minutes to get to Moore's Pocket from Yellowthread Street.

11.37.

He heard Kyle-Foxby shriek a single word on the telephone that chilled him to the bone. The word was 'Bomb.'

It was in Moore's Pocket. He had worked it out. It was going off in no more than twenty-eight minutes.

O'Yee said, 'Where? *Where* in Moore's Pocket?'

It was Kyle Foxby's greatest triumph. He knew.

He knew precisely.

On the phone, not knowing, in that awful, heart-stopping moment what to do, O'Yee said in a gasp, 'Oh my God – Harry! *NO!*'

He saw a muzzle. It was behind the door, coming out. It was not a Consulate at all. It was – it was God knew what.

11.39 exactly.

Feiffer, drawing his revolver and crouching down, yelled as above him the metal detector began buzzing and, somewhere in the building, alarms began going off, 'Move one inch behind that door and – so help me – everyone inside that bloody room is *dead.*'

His hand holding the gun was trembling.

Outside, there was only the sound of the traffic.

His hand holding his revolver was dripping perspiration.

11.39 in Moore's Pocket – *exactly.*

There was a rustling, a whispered exchange of voices, and then, slowly, cautiously, an inch at a time, whoever was behind it began to push open the door under Feiffer's outstretched gun hand to face him.

14

The traffic was building up. At 11.42, reaching its noontime peak, it was becoming transformed into a single, moving block of cars and trucks and buses. The traffic lights at the end of Khartoum Street were gone — somehow it was still working. Somehow, at the far extremity of the system, synchronized lights on other streets were holding it, organizing it, and it was flowing. It was still working. Between each car and truck and bus and taxi there was a measured space: three feet, maybe less, never more — the system was still balanced, organized — it was speeding up, getting faster and faster, still holding the gap. At the far end of Moore's Pocket where it joined Khartoum Street, Kyle-Foxby, out of his Land Rover, glanced up and down the street. There were no coloured flashing lights, no graphics, no computer-enhanced lines — it was real. Buildings, sidewalks, vehicles: he smelled the carbon monoxide and saw people inside all the vehicles looking at him. It was *real*.

All it was going to take was one more bomb. He knew where. He glanced up and down the street and looked for lines and flashing lights on a computer.

There were none. He saw people. It was real. He heard the sound of engines, of horns, of gears changing. He saw people inside all the vehicles: faces — looking out at him. It was *real*. He could find nothing.

All it was going to take was one more bomb. He knew where it was going to be placed.

He could find nothing. There were no lines or lights. Running, moving east, he looked up at the buildings. They were different, higgledy-piggledy: they were not clean, neat, evenly lit lines on his screen – they were tumbledown and paint peeling and unmarked. Time, time . . . He looked at his watch. 11.45. There was no time. He saw, for a moment, at the far end of the street, Auden and Spencer and O'Yee at their car and, glancing up, trying to work out where he was, he began to go towards them shouting.

At the car at the East Yellowthread Street end of Moore's Pocket, Auden, drawing his gun, shouted, 'Where the hell is it?' He saw O'Yee shake his head and reach in to settle the dog on the back seat. Auden, waving the gun, looking up and down the street, yelled above the noise of the traffic, 'The bomber's bloody office. Where the hell is it?' Records hadn't known. He looked up, saw the building in front of him was an agency for a Singapore Import Export firm and shouted, 'This isn't it. All Records knew was that it was somewhere in this street.' He saw Spencer flicking his way through the car's business office directory. Spencer was shaking his head. Auden, seeing the effect the gun had on people in the passing cars and holding it down by his side, yelled, 'Well? Well?'

'It's not here.' Half in half out of the car, Spencer, riffling pages, shouted back, 'It's not here. It's not listed under his name.' He looked up and down the street and saw only the traffic. 'It has to be here.' It wasn't. He attacked the book again. 'I can't find it anywhere.' He saw O'Yee trying to crane above the traffic to see both sides of the street, 'Christopher?'

'No.' In the car, the dog was becoming restless. O'Yee, reaching in and giving it a quick calming pat, said urgently, 'No, I can't –' Wherever Feiffer was he wasn't on the street. O'Yee, shaking his head, said, 'No, I can't see him anywhere.' He heard the dog start to throw itself against the half closed window of the car to get out and he said, 'Hey, dog –'

163

'The bloody bomber's got his office in this goddamned street.' Taller than O'Yee, still clutching the gun, Auden tried to see above the moving wall of traffic. It was accelerating, blocking, getting denser. He smelled the carbon monoxide. Auden, on tip toes, craning his neck to see the other side of the street, yelled, 'Jesus Christ, he's here. He's here somewhere in this bloody street and I can't see him.' The buildings were all worn and faded. Their signs, once painted in huge letters on their sides, were now only shadows. All the names of all the new establishments were engraved on nothing more than little brass plates. They were unreadable. Auden, hopping up and down, said as the dog threw itself against the window of the car and began howling, 'Shut up! Shut up and let me think!' He saw O'Yee looking for Feiffer. Auden, reaching down and taking Spencer by the shoulder as he flicked urgently through the directory, yelled, 'Well? Well?'

'Nothing! I can't find it! I can't find the number at all!'

'*Harry!*' It was useless. O'Yee's voice was taken by the traffic. He might have as well been whispering. '*Harry!*' He heard the dog's howling turn into a frantic barking. It was 11.44.

O'Yee, desperate, yelled at the top of his voice, 'HARRY! HARRY *FEIFFER!*'

He saw it. For a moment all the lines and lights on the computer accorded with reality and he saw where the bomb was. It was in a building at the end of the street – it was exactly, perfectly in synch with the simulation – exactly, precisely right. It was at the far end of the street. Kyle-Foxby, running, trying to find a break in the traffic, yelled, 'There! It's there! The last bomb! It's there!'

No one could hear him. The traffic was flowing faster and faster. Somehow, as noon approached, it was being released, building up in intensity, getting faster and faster as –

He saw it begin to happen. He saw the gap between the vehicles close. He heard gears change up. Kyle-Foxby, halted, stopped, marooned on the wrong side of the road, said suddenly, 'Oh my God!' He understood. He understood what they were doing: all of it – the closing of the streets, the meters all gone in General Gordon Street to speed the one way flow up to a rush, the build-up in all the feeder streets to the flyover, the bulge in Moore's Pocket that just for a few hundred feet ran free and wide and open as the drivers, in a last glorious liberated burst of speed accelerated towards the flyover – he understood it. He knew exactly what they were doing. He saw the final point for the bomb. He understood the system. He honed its location. He understood the plan, all the people and cars and vehicles in the street, all fitting into place in the jigsaw – he knew exactly what was going to happen and he knew exactly when.

He looked at his watch. 11.45. He had only minutes remaining. Fighting, signalling his way through the traffic, searching for gaps that closed second by second, Kyle-Foxby, running towards the last bomb, yelled at the top of his voice to no one, to nothing in the roaring and frenzy as, all along the street, the cars and vehicles, going towards their last moments, accelerated to be free, 'No. Listen. *STOP.*'

It was gone. Spencer, getting out, had opened the rear car door just a fraction of an inch and the dog was gone. In its entire life only two people had ever loved it and, above all the stinks and smells of the street, it sensed where the other one had gone. Bounding, seeing Feiffer for an instant through the door of the two storey building at the corner of the street where a flag blew, the dog went at full tilt towards him barking and yelping with pleasure.

In the hallway of the building, backing out into the steps, Feiffer ordered the two Europeans in the tiled hallway, 'Drop the guns! Take the gunbelts off and let them fall to the floor!'

Outside the traffic was at top peak: he could hardly hear himself think. He saw the taller of the two men hesitate for a moment and, drawing back the hammer of his Detective Special and aiming it between the man's eyes, Feiffer snarled,

'No second chance! Drop it now or I'll kill you where you stand!' They were staring at his own holster on his belt. They saw the loops of spare cartridges. They were gun experts. They saw the Colt Detective Special police issue .38. Feiffer, his hand trembling, yelled, 'Police! Do what you're told!'

They were South Africans. The voice that came out of the shorter man was pure Johannesburg-accented English. The shorter man, nodding hard to his companion, ordered him, 'Do it, Henrik!' He had his own hands out in front of him, palms open. 'Man, we're Security! We're on your side!' Behind him, the door to the little room was open. On the floor there were cardboard cartons of equipment and bits and pieces of what looked like burglar alarms spilling out of them. The shorter man, his hands still out and open, said in appeal, 'We're official Security! We were watching you because we –'

It was no Consulate. It was a shell. Apart from the room and the hallway there was nothing. It was a watching post. The taller man, unbuckling his gun, said in a snarl, 'Shut up.' The taller man said quickly, 'We've got nothing to say.' It was no Consulate. There was no police licence for the weapons. The taller man, turning back to the room a fraction and seeing the muzzle of his Sterling sub-machine gun sticking out from under one of the boxes, said tightly, 'We've got nothing to say.'

'Who the hell are you people?'

'*Nothing!* Nothing to say!' There were bits and pieces of alarms and devices all over the floor in various states of repair. The taller man, glancing back at them, said formally, 'We wish to stand on our rights and –'

They were all dead. In Sepoy Street they had all been dead like blackened logs. He had found a slipper, embroidered with Shensi needlework. It had belonged to someone, one of the dead. Feiffer, taking a step forward, said warningly, 'Listen –'

'Nothing to say, man! *Nothing to say!*'

They were all dead, all of them. Feiffer, moving a little forward, feeling a muscle somewhere in his face beginning to go, said, in a whisper, 'No, that's just not good enough –' He had the gun out in front of him in his hand. He felt his hand dripping perspiration, trembling. Feiffer, advancing, said, shaking his head, 'No . . . no . . .'

'Man!' The shorter man, stepping back, seeing what was going to happen, said, 'No!' He was shaking with fear. He knew guns. He saw the muzzle of the .38 moving, changing direction, going towards his gut. The shorter man, shaking his head, said desperately, 'No! *Don't!*'

He was going to be killed. The dog was in the midst of the moving traffic, running in and out of it trying to find a direct route to the building and any second he was going to be run down and killed. O'Yee running after him, yelled back to Auden and Spencer, 'It's Feiffer! He knows where Feiffer is!' He saw Spencer throw the directory back into the open car and yank at Auden as Auden began running after him. 11.48. There was no time.

O'Yee, turning, losing the dog for a second, yelled back as an order, 'No! No! Find the bomber! Find his bloody address! *Find Henry Yu!*' He saw, as he ran, a brass nameplate. It was Yu's office. O'Yee, passing it, yelled, 'There! There! *Go!*'

It was Yu. There, on the floor of the room, spread out, there were boxes of alarms with Yu's name stencilled on them. It had been Yu all along. He had seen him. In Sepoy Street, watching, Feiffer had seen him touch the weeping Collins on the arm and look concerned.

He had been concerned that Collins, unable to bear the killing, was going to tell him something. In the hallway, Feiffer, standing stock still, said in a voice that for a moment seemed to come not from him, but from someone else, 'You people are guarding something and if you don't tell me what it is in the next two seconds so help me God one of you is going to die.' It was all gone, all the control – it was all too long and too late and now there was nothing more than all the dead in all the streets and – Feiffer, gasping for breath, said tightly, 'Do you understand me? You people know what all the deaths are all about and if one of you doesn't tell me I'm going to gut shoot the pair of you and then –' He saw the shorter man's eyes bulge in fear, '*People have been bloody killed and you know why!*' Behind him, he heard a sound, like an animal running. He heard a slavering noise. Feiffer, the gun shaking in his hand like a leaf, shrieked, 'It's bloody Henry Yu, isn't it? He's the one behind it! *Isn't he?*' They were both terrified, struck dumb. Feiffer, his finger beginning to press on the trigger, shrieked, 'Isn't he? WHAT THE HELL ARE YOU PEOPLE GUARDING?'

It was Yu. It was Henry Yu. Once, a long time ago when he had been a Sergeant in the Bomb Squad, he had met a refugee from his old province and married her as a defence – a show – against his homosexuality. It had done him no good. Nothing had done him any good. Against the Americans, against the employers of his lover Nonte, nothing had done him any good. At the closed door to his office, Auden, the giant gun in his hand, yelled at the moving shadow going to ground behind an alarm strewn desk in the half light, 'Yu! Stand still or I'll blow your fucking head off!' He saw Spencer with his gun out a fraction of a second behind him. He saw something glint behind the desk: a badge or a gun or a – Auden, cocking the big revolver and ready to kill, yelled, 'One move and you're –' He said suddenly, 'What the hell are you doing here?'

He saw who it was.

Auden, stunned, said with the gun falling away to his side, 'How the hell did you get here?'

In the hallway of the building, O'Yee, seeing what was a second away from happening, yelled, 'Harry, no!' The dog was beside him, looking confused. There were too many people. O'Yee, pushing it out of the way, reaching out for Feiffer, shaking his head, said warningly, 'Harry, no, don't . . . We know who it is!'

'It's Henry Yu.'

'Yes! Auden and Spencer –' O'Yee saw the gun shaking in Feiffer's hand. It was cocked. All it was going to take was . . .

O'Yee, going forward, reaching out for the gun, said over and over, 'No, Harry, no . . . no!'

It was Technical Inspector Matthews of the Bomb Squad. In Yu's office, having found nothing, Matthews said with a shake of his head, 'He's gone. He's not here.' He saw the gun in Auden's hand, 'We're too fucking late. He's gone.' He saw Spencer looking confused.

Matthews, rubbing his hand on his grey overalls where he had his service revolver strapped on, said with a twisted look on his face, 'I looked him up in the phone book! After I taught him everything he knows about killing people with bombs he went into the fucking burglar alarm business!' He had something in his other hand. It was something he had found on one of the desks when he had searched it.

Matthews, blinking back something in his eyes, holding up the object for them to see, said in a strangled whisper, 'I found this.' It was something so small, so insignificant that in the poor light, it was almost invisible.

Matthews, coming closer, holding it out for them to see, said as an order, 'Look! Fucking *look at it*!'

It was a single piece of twisted copper wire.

It was the way he, Matthews, had always made his detonating wires.

It was what he had taught Yu to do.

It was no blank, no exhibit, no academic study.

It was death.

Matthews, thrusting it at them, still blinking, his hands tight together as fists, ordered them in a fury, '*Look at it!*'

There was nothing in Moore's Pocket.

There was a television camera and armed men overseeing — overseeing what?

There was nothing. There was only a one roomed, glass-doored, non-high risk Chartered Securities Company across the road.

There was nothing. There was Yu. There was Nonte. There

was Collins. There was a man who knew the streets and a man who knew how the streets were made.

In Moore's Pocket there was nothing.

In Moore's . . . *Pocket* . . . there was . . .

They were South Africans. There were men with automatic weapons and a belief in their own legality.

They were . . .

Pocket. Pocket. Moore's Pocket.

There was . . .

Sir Hercules Moore. Once, in that street, when it had been an oasis of calm, Sir Hercules Moore . . .

Moore's Pocket.

Moore had died a suicide, a bankrupt.

There was a camera watching across the street. It was watching the Chartered Securities Company. There was an official flag. There was – 'Man, don't . . . !' He heard the accent.

Nonte. Nonte with all his old books and records and charts of the place. Moore's . . . *pocket*. It was a vault. Somewhere beneath the street there was Sir Hercules Moore's pocket – his real pocket.

It was a vault.

South Africa.

They were safe, those two. The taller one was going to stand on his rights because he was –

He knew. In the hallway, suddenly, Feiffer knew. He heard O'Yee say in a whisper, 'Harry . . .'

Henry Yu knew what was down there because he had installed all the alarms and Nonte, he knew because –

Behind him, O'Yee said urgently, 'Harry, Nonte and Yu are lovers. The Chinese woman who was living with Collins was Yu's ex-wife . . .'

He knew because his friend Yu had asked him to look it up and his other friend Collins, obligingly, knowing all the streets – without any trouble at all – had known exactly what to go for with the bombs to achieve the desired result.

A pocket. A vault.

There was nothing worth having in Moore's Pocket.

Like hell there wasn't.

He saw the shorter man sweat. Feiffer, bringing the gun up to cover him, now with no intention of pulling the trigger, knowing it all, said quietly, 'It's de Beers, isn't it? It's the storage vault for de Beers' South African diamond operation, isn't it?'

He saw the taller man blanch. 'It's the storage point for all the diamond markets of Asia, isn't it? It's below the Chartered Securities Company across the street, *isn't it*? And it's been there since about 1907, hasn't it? It's where de Beers' store the diamonds they let onto the Asian market a few at a time.'

That was what they had killed all those people for. It almost, in that second, seemed worth it. Feiffer, at last, having found it, having understood it, having made some sense of all the death and slaughter, knowing he was right, shrieked above the sound of the traffic, *'ISN'T IT?'*

It was noon. It was the last moment.

It was a gridlock. It was the final, ultimate traffic nightmare: the total, complete shutdown when no vehicle, nothing – nothing at all – could move a single inch in any direction. One bomb. All it was going to take was one bomb and everything, everything would stop.

In the street, Kyle-Foxby, running towards the building with the flag flying on it, saw Auden and Spencer coming towards him with another man in coveralls. It was a gridlock. It was seconds away. When it happened, when all over the system in one sudden exploding instant, it happened, all there would be on the streets would be death and chaos. He knew where it was: the final bomb. He had worked it out. It was in the building with the flag, on the corner of the street. Kyle-Foxby, out of breath, pointing to it, gasped, 'There! There! It's in there!'

'*Yes!*' In the hallway, the shorter man yelled, 'Yes! It's de Beers!' He heard someone yell from the roadway, 'It's a bomb! It's in there!' and, glancing back into the room, seeing the sealed boxes the man from the alarm company had delivered that morning with strict instructions that they should not be opened, the shorter man, his position of trust all shot to hell, yelled in appeal, 'For God's sake, save the diamonds!' Forgetting the gun, he began to run back into the room. He felt his friend only a moment behind him. He yelled, going for the cartons, 'Henrik —!' He yelled in Afrikaans, 'Help me!'

He got his hands onto the nearest carton. It was heavy. He began to lift it up and, at noon plus one second exactly, as inside the box the electrical timer reached the zenith of its climb towards a single twisted copper wire and sent a charge of five volts directly, shatteringly into its chemical detonator, he was lost in a blast that, simultaneously, tore him and everything inside the little, secret back room to pieces.

15

It had gone. It had happened. The front of the building had gone in a single annihilating blast and spilled out onto the road and all over the system it was happening and everything was ruined, going crazy, concertinaing. From across the road at the Chartered Securities Company there was the sound of gunfire and then, a moment later, a car skidding, on fire, hit the side of the plate glass window and burned. There were screams. He saw people trapped. It was stopping, colliding, crashing – all the traffic along all the back-up roads, led piece by piece to the moment – directed, signalled, *aimed* by all the closed and cordoned off roads was coming to a halt, being jammed. It was a gridlock. It was the ultimate nightmare where, caught up, locked together, crashing into each other and burning, pumping out their poison gas from their exhausts, no vehicle could move an inch in any direction.

Half way out on the road, Kyle-Foxby, diving away as the burning car slewed at him with all the people inside screaming, saw for a moment a bus seem to take off, rise up on its rear wheels as something hit it from behind, then, as it jammed hard against a car in front of it, all the people inside begin rushing for the doors and the windows to get out.

He heard an engine roar as along the sidewalk – all jammed with cars – someone in a Mercedes taxi tried to reverse and, in a pall of blue exhaust smoke, crashed again and again into the car behind him. All the doors on all the cars were jammed hard by other cars – there was nowhere to manoeuvre. He heard more revving and then, as someone somewhere panicked, a terrible crash as again and again, demented, they rammed each other to get out. He heard the screaming. The smoke – the carbon monoxide was rising. Kyle-Foxby, getting to his feet, dodging, shrieking above the chaos, yelled, 'No! No! Listen! *Stop!*' He saw Feiffer and O'Yee on the steps of the blown-down building trying to move through a billowing wall of masonry dust and exhaust fumes onto the sidewalk and he yelled, 'Look out,' as someone on a motorcycle, somehow having turned in the street and going the wrong way, careered past them and seemed to disappear under a truck. The truck was revving, its wheels smoking and on fire as they spun against the unmovable force of a car wedged in front of it. He saw the motorcyclist raise his hand for a moment and then, in the fumes, like a drowning man, he was gone.

It was a gridlock. It was the ultimate nightmare. Kyle-Foxby, dodging, weaving, trying to find something to do, yelled first in English and then in Cantonese, 'No! Stop! *Turn off your engines!*'

'Boss! Boss!' Caught up half way across the road in the traffic, Auden, wrenching the motorcyclist out from under the truck and shoving him away, yelled to Feiffer, 'It's Yu! He's in the building across the street!' He heard gunfire. For an instant he got a break between two cars and saw someone running inside the bank or whatever it was. It was the Hong Bay Chartered Securities Company. Through the haze he saw their sign. The man was a clerk or a manager. There was someone behind him. He was going for the glass doors. There were shots and then the man, cut down, fell over, and disappeared. In the bank, running, the shotgun still in his hand, he saw a man in a dustmask. He paused, seemed to shout at someone and then, as above Auden's head someone in the bus smashed a window to escape, there was a shower of glass and Auden, ducking, covering his head, yelled, 'Bill! Bill!' He saw Spencer with his gun out, looking first one way and then the other, trying to decide about the bus. Spencer was below the bus shouting at people, telling them to stay inside. Everywhere the engines were roaring. Auden, seeing Feiffer and O'Yee for an instant, yelled, 'Harry! Here! They're over here!'

'Christopher!' At what was left of the side of the Consulate, Feiffer, trying to locate him, yelled, 'Christopher, for Christ's sake get back inside the doorway!' He saw the traffic going mad, slewing, fighting, filling the street with gas. He saw O'Yee, for an instant, down on his hands and knees under a car reaching for the dog, '*Christopher!*'

In the street all the alarms had gone off. Across the road the car against the Chartered Securities Company was burning. He saw, from somewhere, Kyle-Foxby at it with a hand-held extinguisher. He saw O'Yee wrench at something under the car. Feiffer yelled, 'Christopher! They're in the bloody diamond company!'

It was all solid, jammed; all the cars and vehicles were roaring their engines and jamming hard up against each other – they were filling up the sidewalks and wedging against all the buildings, caught, stuck, moulded into the bricks. Feiffer, getting down, grabbing O'Yee by the scruff of the neck and pulling him up, yelled, 'We have to go across the cars.' He saw Auden and Spencer caught in the midst of the careering, jamming vehicles. He saw people inside all the vehicles hammering at their windows to get out, 'Christopher, we have to go across the top of the cars!' He saw O'Yee look wildly back towards what was left of the building behind him. Feiffer, shaking his head, yelled, 'No, they're both dead!' He had O'Yee by the shoulder, pulling him backwards. 'We have to go across the top of the cars! Do you understand? *Across the top of the cars!*' He saw Spencer clambering up to the top of the bus from the bonnet of a car and, waving at him, catching his attention for a moment, Feiffer yelled, 'No! For God's sake don't turn the people loose on the street – there's nowhere to go!' He heard sirens. They would get no further than Yellow-

175

thread Street. The gridlock would see to that. That was what it was all about. Feiffer, pushing O'Yee towards a wedged truck outside the smashed Consulate building, yelled into the chaos, 'Don't let the people in the cars loose on the street!'

'Do it! Do it!' In the basement of the Hong Bay Chartered Securities Company, Nonte, with the charges all in place against the massive steel vault door, running back up the stairs, shrieked to Yu, 'Now! Do it!' He saw the wires snaking back down to the vault behind him. It was a shaped charge: all the force was going to slice through the steel locks. 'Don't wait for me! Do it!' He saw the two Wing brothers running in from upstairs with their pistols out. 'Henry, do it now!' He made the stairs two at a time. He saw, for a moment, his lover's eyes looking terrified for him and he shouted, 'Henry, I'm all right! Do it now!'

He saw Yu press down on the detonating plunger.

He was running, virtually leaping from car to car. They were made of tinplate, of what felt like cardboard. Their bonnets with each pressure seemed to crumple. Auden was up on top of a Volkswagen truck, crawling across the roof to another, a higher truck.

Feiffer saw O'Yee near Spencer, running across a series of flat roofed taxis, caving them in as he went. Below the roofs, under them, there were people hammering to get out. He heard the screaming. There was glass smashing and the sound of Kyle-Foxby's fire extinguisher as he flooded the burning car at the Securities Company with foam. Everywhere, everywhere there were people screaming. Briefly, for a second, he was lost behind a truck. Feiffer, looking around, losing his balance and almost falling, hearing the screams of the people, yelled, 'Where are they? Where the hell are they?' He heard, deep under the ground, a thundering explosion and, sliding along the roof of a car, taking cover, got his gun out and tried to see the Securities Company.

All around him the alarms on all the buildings were ringing.

He could hear them even above the screaming. He saw Spencer on the bus and yelled, 'Bill! Bill! Leave them! They're going to come out of the diamond company with guns!' He saw Spencer hesitate, 'Leave it! *Leave it!*'

'Cops!' They were coming across the cars. At the top of the stairs to the vault, one of the Wings yelled down in Cantonese, 'Cops! You said we'd have time! There are cops out there!' The explosion had torn the six foot square vault door off its hinges. He saw Nonte and Yu at the opening filling knapsacks with diamonds. He saw them glitter. He saw his own brother behind them with diamonds all over his lap, ramming them into two knapsacks and for a moment his eyes bulged. There were millions – the entire floor was alive with light. He turned, saw a policeman in uniform only feet from the front door with a fire extinguisher, and he yelled down in terror, 'Hurry! Hurry!' Nonte had said there would have been no one – that the gridlock of wrecked, stopped cars was going to give them all the time in the world. Outside, everywhere, swarming across the tops of the wrecked and stopped cars, there were cops. He looked back and saw a red-faced European carrying a gigantic Colt Python leap like some sort of gazelle across onto the roof of a flat topped van and, not knowing which way to look, Wing yelled, 'Come on! Come on!' He saw Nonte's face for an instant. He saw his eyes. He yelled down, 'What are we going to do?'

He saw Nonte's eyes.

He saw his face.

Yu, coming up the stairs, the shotgun in his free hand, swinging the knapsack of diamonds over his shoulder in a single movement, yelled, 'What do you think we're going to do?' Behind Wing the two dead clerks from the front office were lying in pools of blood. Yu, glancing at them for only a second, shrieked, looking out, seeing Feiffer, 'Kill them! We're going to kill them!' He saw Kyle-Foxby suddenly at the plate glass window moving around with something big and heavy in his hand and, shooting from the hip, Yu blew down the window and sent him spinning. Behind him, he saw Nonte and the other Wing coming up the stairs pulling at their dust masks. Everywhere there were diamonds. Yu, slipping a spare round into the magazine of his shotgun, ready to escape, yelled, 'Now! Come on! Now! *Out! Out!*'

He saw him. He saw him fall. Feiffer, sliding across a bonnet and finding nowhere to set his feet down, called out, spreadeagled, 'You! Kyle-Foxby!' He saw the man caught between the burning car and a stoved-in Mini scrabbling to get out from under the glass. 'Stay there! Don't move! We'll get to you!' He was stuck. Crawling, clambering, trying to get a hand hold, Feiffer went on his stomach over the bonnet and tried to find a space to get back down onto the road. There was no space. For a moment, as he swivelled, his gun hand turned and covered people in the car in front of him. He saw their faces. They were like concentration camp victims being gassed, caught inside the death chamber of the car, their fists smashing at the windscreen, unable to break it, panicking, shrieking. He saw Kyle-Foxby, somehow, stand up against the burned out car, his face and hands covered in blood. He saw him stagger. Feiffer, trying to get to him, seeing briefly O'Yee go down between two cars for his cursed dog and disappear, called out into the smoke, 'Spencer! Auden!' He saw Yu and Nonte and the two Wings inside the bank. 'Christopher! Cover Kyle-Foxby! They're coming out!'

To hell with him. To hell with his criminals and his deaths and his killings and his ambulances with dying coppers inside with their hands blown off. There were people in cars – traffic – there were things he knew how to do.

Kyle-Foxby, pushing the glass aside, feeling it slice deeper into his hand, shaking his head, said to no one, 'No! *No!*' There was space between the cars. He got to his feet and saw, for the first time, all the way along the street what had happened. He saw traffic. He saw his work. He saw, for an instant, someone under a car crawling towards him with his gun out and, still shaking his head, in full uniform, swinging himself up between two cars like a gymnast, got himself up onto the roof of a Ford and began moving quickly away towards the centre of the jam to get people organized.

'Harry!' Under the car, searching for the dog, he saw a movement. They were coming out of the bank. Above him, O'Yee could hear the screaming from the people in the cars. He heard a series of hard, heavy thumps, as, not stopping, running from car to car, Auden and Spencer went across the road above him. He saw something in the bank: a glint of something – a weapon. He was crawling out from under the car to a gap. He smelled rubber burning. He was almost under the burning car. O'Yee, twisting, still looking for his dog, looked up and saw, in the most awful moment of his life, the barrel of a pistol only inches from his face.

'Phil!' He was there. He was across the road, but too far down. Spencer, seeing Auden reach the wall of the building next to the bank, saw a dust masked man at the bank with a pistol in his hand. He saw the pistol pointing downwards, aiming at someone. It was O'Yee. He knew it was. It was O'Yee. Spencer, slipping and falling as he tried to get closer on top of a car, yelled, 'Phil! Get a shot in! Can't you see him? Get a shot in!' He saw the man with the pistol touch for a moment at his dusk mask and then, holding his weapon up and out in one extended hand like an Olympic pistol shooter, aiming without compunction for the head, Spencer fired twice and blew the side of his neck and half his shoulder away.

'It's my brother!' The other Wing, half way out of the smashed glass doors, turning, trying to find Yu and Nonte, yelled in Cantonese, 'It's my brother! He's –' He saw Spencer scrabble up to the bonnet of a car and he got his revolver and tried to take aim. He felt Yu and Nonte behind him. He heard a click as Nonte cocked a sub-machine gun. He yelled – He felt a blast as Nonte let fly an entire magazine and deafened him.

179

'*Bill!*' He was at the wrong angle. At the wall, Auden, unable to get a second shot, saw the bullets punch the cars around Spencer to pieces. Inside the cars there were people screaming, being killed. He saw Spencer go over. Running, leaping from car to car, bringing the big Python up, Auden shooting wildly, smashed the door jamb around Nonte's head to pieces, and, reloading as he went, made a leap across an abyss between two cars to get a final killing shot in at anything that moved.

He missed. In a single terrible moment, he knew he had missed the second car. He felt his foot touch the bonnet and slide off. He knew —

Falling, going down feet first between the two cars, seeing all his spare ammunition cascading down around him like glittering confetti, Auden, in Nonte's exact line of fire, saw the dust masked man bring up the reloaded machine gun and draw back the bolt.

It was jammed. The magazine of his gun had only gone half way into its housing and when he drew back the bolt the round coming off the top had wedged itself into the breech and it was jammed. Nonte, stepping back, yelled in English, 'It won't shoot!' He saw Auden caught between two cars. He saw his head and shoulders. He saw him grasping desperately for something on the ground he was never going to reach and, thrusting the surviving Wing brother out in front of him, giving him his chance, Nonte yelled at him, 'Kill him! Kill him!'

He was going to die. Any second now he was going to die. He was going to die alone. Auden, caught, ignoramus that he was, was going to be slaughtered like a steer in an abattoir, alone, without friends. The cartridges for his gun were on the ground by his feet. He could see them. They glittered dully in the rising fumes. And he was going to die. Auden, grimacing, wanting to shut his eyes, but afraid to, shaking his head, said softly, over and over, 'Bill . . . Bill . . .' He saw Spencer up and alive on the top of a car, coming towards him. He saw one of the dust masked men at the doorway raise his pistol. He saw —

He saw Spencer suddenly turn and shoot. He saw – He saw bits and pieces of glass fly off around the dust masked man's head. He saw – He felt Spencer's hands on his shoulders. He saw – He felt – The man at the door had his gun up again. He saw –

He saw O'Yee from nowhere up on his feet between two cars, shouting, stopping, warning the man with the gun. He saw –

He felt Spencer's arms under his shoulder. Auden, gasping, grateful, said, 'Thanks. Thanks. Thanks. Thanks –' He saw his friend Spencer smile. He said over and over, 'Thanks. Thanks. Thanks –' He saw O'Yee. He saw the man with the gun turn to face him. He saw O'Yee fire a single shot and take his chest away. Auden, gasping, sobbing, said over and over, 'Thanks, oh, thanks – oh, thanks . . '

He was working it, getting it right. Out in the road, at the bus, getting between the vehicles the uniform was getting it right. He had his whistle out. He was blowing it over and over, attracting their attention. Kyle-Foxby, all his buttons shining, touching at his uniform, his face and hands still covered in blood, *showing his authority*, a bit at a time, was getting it right.

One by one, as he ordered them, they were all turning off their engines. He could see the exhaust fumes abating.

One by one . . .

One by one . . .

He was doing what he did best.

Kyle-Foxby, moving, running, weaving, getting somehow between the cars and buses and objects of his life's study, seeing for the first time people, blowing at his whistle to attract their attention – to save them – a little at a time was getting it right.

He was there, in the corridor. At the rear of the Chartered Securities Company, at the already unlocked door, Matthews, waiting, saw him. He saw Henry Yu. He saw him stop and see him. He heard him say, 'Bob! No!'

He saw him see that Matthews' gun was still in its holster.

He waited. Matthews waited.

They were making it, getting there. Like an army, they were overrunning the bank. It was no good. It was all gone. The gridlock was supposed to stop anyone getting to the street when the alarms went off. They were already there. Nonte looked around and Yu was gone and he was alone and his gun was jammed and all over the street, coming from everywhere, Feiffer and his people were overrunning him and there was nowhere to go. His lover had gone. Yu, leaving him the way he had left him to kill Collins' woman, was gone and now, with everything in his life destroyed, there was nowhere to go.

In the corridor, Matthews said quietly, 'Go for it, Henry.' He nodded at the shotgun in Yu's hand. 'Go for it.' He had taught him everything he knew. Matthews, his face twisted in hate, said softly, 'Go for it.'

'I can't outdraw you, Bob. I've seen you do it on the range. I can't –'

'Yes, you can.' Matthews, standing easily, said quietly, 'Yes, you can. Sergeant, you outdid me in everything else – in killing people and setting bombs and twisting little bits of wire – so I don't see why you can't outdo me now. After all, you've got the drop.' His face was bland. All his life all he had ever known were weapons. Matthews, his hand well away from his re-volver holster, said quietly, 'Go on, Sergeant, make a try for it.'

He was there: Nonte. He saw him. He was a little behind the body of one of the Wing brothers, working at the gun. Getting there, making it, coming closer, Feiffer saw only Nonte. He was there. It was him. Under the white dust mask as he cocked at the machine gun the way he had cocked at the shotgun to kill the girl in Collins' apartment, it was Nonte. He saw him working at the gun. He saw him. It was Nonte. It was all too late. Shensi work: a single black slipper with a Shensi embroidered lotus pattern on it – all unidentifiable, all gone, all blasted to valueless insignificance, all the people in Sepoy Street all dead and blackened like logs. It was Nonte. All along, with his borrowed maps and his old books and his eyes narrowed, searching for ways to kill and profit, it had been Nonte. He saw him look up. He saw him with the useless, jammed gun in his hand. His hands were shaking. On the bonnet of a car, standing stock still, Feiffer's hands were shaking. He saw him. He saw Nonte. He saw the jammed gun in his hands.

It was all, all –

He saw him look up.

He saw his eyes.

The gun, in his hands, was jammed and useless. He saw Nonte take off the dust mask and smile to surrender, to give up, to take life and jail.

He saw him smile.

He saw, again, the little Shensi work slipper.

He saw him.

'Try for it!' In the corridor, Matthews, stepping forward, yelled, 'You dirty little traitorous thieving bastard, make a try for it!' Outside, he could hear engines on all the cars stopping. 'Try for it! Make a try for it the way you made a try for everything else I ever taught you!' Matthews, his hand falling to the butt of his gun, yelled, 'Now! Make a try for it! You've got the drop on me with the fucking shotgun – make a try for it! You've been right every other time with all the things I taught you, so be right this time!' He ordered the hesitating man, 'Do it! It's the only chance you've got!'

He saw him. He saw Nonte.

Taking aim, somehow, somehow finding it in himself, Feiffer, with a single round, shot him dead where he stood.

*

'Bob —'

'Bob — *please*!' He was crying, weeping.

In the corridor, Technical Inspector Matthews, going forward, in all his life with all the weapons Man had ever devised, never once having harmed a living human soul, watching as Yu let the shotgun fall to the floor, went forward with his handcuffs.

He was an artist, a technician. He touched for a moment at his holstered revolver. As always, it was unloaded.

Like the man from Traffic outside in the street, he was a man who loved not people, but machines.

He never fought for people.

In his own, mechanical, organized, perfect world, he never saw the need.

'Harry . . .'

In the street, Feiffer said quietly, 'Yes.' He looked at the injured dog in O'Yee's arms and smiled. The alarms had all been turned off and up and down Moore's Pocket all the engines of the cars and vehicles were silent and the people inside were waiting quietly for the sirens they could hear coming. Feiffer, patting at the dog, said in a whisper, 'What's your landlord going to say?'

'I don't know.' He had the dog cradled gently. It was a dog that spoke no languages at all. It merely looked up at him with love. O'Yee, squeezing it a little, said with a shrug, 'My kids have always wanted a dog. I guess we can always move somewhere where they allow pets.'

At the smashed door of the Hong Bay Chartered Securities Company Nonte was lying in a pool of blood with his eyes open staring at the jammed gun. Feiffer, glancing away, said, 'Sure.' He saw Spencer and Auden against a building waiting for the ambulance. They were saying nothing. Feiffer said with a nod, 'Yep, everyone needs a friend.'

He saw, in his mind, for a moment, the little slipper with the Shensi work embroidered so carefully and lovingly upon it.

'*You are fatter . . .*'

He heard words, whispers, sounds. He had no idea where they came from.

Looking down at the dog, wondering, Feiffer touched at his face, and found that — soundlessly, pointlessly, for no reason at all — he seemed to be weeping.

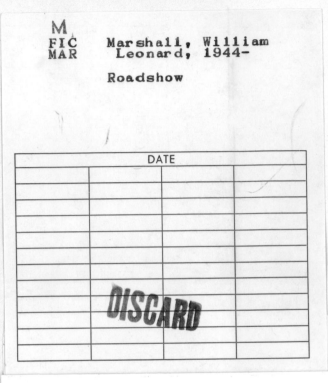

DATE			